The People
From the Sea

The People
From the Sea

Velda Johnston

Dodd, Mead & Company · New York

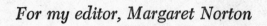

For my editor, Margaret Norton

*The People
From the Sea*

Chapter 1

Unless it has burned down at sometime during these past months, or been swept away by one of the storms that often howl across eastern Long Island during January and February, the house still stands behind the dune that separates it from the winter-empty beach and the Atlantic beyond. In all probability, next June some temporary tenant—but not I, not again!—will brew coffee on the cheap enamel kitchen stove with its network of fine cracks. Perhaps children will race up the veranda's broad wooden steps to leave sandy footprints on the straw living-room rug. And in the afternoons the glasses of cocktail guests will make additional rings on the walnut coffee table and the lid of the ancient console phonograph.

But of one thing I feel sure: Those three who shared the house with me for a time last summer—that handsome trio who some may say had no existence outside my own disordered imagination—will not be there. The sound of the battered upright piano, playing a melody popular more than a quarter of a century ago, will not drift up the staircase at night. Neither I nor anyone else, stepping at dusk from the hall into the shadowy living room, will see Mrs. Woodhull's slender figure at the window facing the dune. And neither I nor anyone will hear her daughter Sheila's silvery laugh, nor see her handsome son Derek, in his uniform from a half-forgotten war, stretch out his hand invitingly while a record of "Harbor Lights" spins—or did it?—on the console's turntable.

No, those three have gone back where they came from, whether it was some corner of my mind or beneath the sparkling sea. But no matter what their reality, or lack of it, the evil in which I became enmeshed because of them was very real, as real as the hands that wrapped around my throat one fog-shrouded afternoon on the beach.

It was David Corway who late last spring persuaded me to rent the house. David was my upstairs neighbor in this West Side Manhattan brownstone. (Fireplaces, twelve-foot-high ceilings, and wainscoted walls, so never mind that on a corner two blocks away, at almost any hour of the day or night, addicts with watering eyes await their pusher.) A junior partner in an architectural firm, David still looked like the Columbia running back he once had been—fairly tall, but with wide shoulders that made him look shorter. Like me, he was divorced, but there the resemblance between us ended. At thirty-two, he seemed more than content with the life of a Manhattan single—discos and theaters on Friday and Saturday nights, summer weekends in the Hamptons and winter weekends in Vermont. But even though my marriage had not been a happy one, I, at twenty-six, felt that my divorce had shunted me, so to speak, onto a sidetrack. There I sat, like an unused railway car, hoping that I could get back onto the rails and resume my real function in life.

Not that I didn't appear, on the surface, to function fairly well. I performed my work adequately—I am an editor of children's books—and when this apartment became available a year ago last October, I summoned up the energy to get through the legal details involved in subletting the Greenwich Village apartment I'd shared with my ex-husband, leasing this new place, and moving my furniture.

A week after I moved in, David and I met, just as in a TV commercial, over the washing machines in the brownstone's basement. Neither of us, however, tried to persuade the other to abandon Brand X for the new, improved washday product. Instead, because I had seen a paperback copy of *Transatlantic Blues* protruding from the hip pocket of his chinos, we discussed

Wilfred Sheed during the wash cycle. Later, while our clothes spin-dried, we talked about where we would like to travel and discovered that we both had an offbeat yen to visit the most remote spot reachable by ship, Little America.

My laundry was dry first. As I folded garments into a wicker basket, he said, "Hey! We haven't introduced ourselves. I'm David Corway."

"Diana Garson." That was my maiden name. Just as I hadn't wanted Gary Durning's alimony, just so I hadn't wanted to hang onto his last name.

We shook hands over my laundry basket. He said, "You don't look like a Diana."

"No?"

"No. A Diana should be tall and haughty, with hair that's either very dark or very blond. Rather small girls with gray eyes and brown hair should always be named Emily."

"Sorry about that."

"Will you have dinner with me tonight, Diana?"

I hesitated. My return to the dating scene hadn't worked out too well. Some of the men who had approached me since my divorce—the overweight forty-seven-year-old bachelor in my firm's accounting department, for instance—had seemed to be too unappealing, either in appearance or manner. And nearly all of the men I had found attractive enough to date had made passes. What's more, they had reacted in a surly fashion when I, still not ready for such involvement, had said no.

Well, this man was attractive indeed and surely must be aware of it, and therefore was almost certain to make a pass. And probably he'd become sullen when I turned him down. I thought of how uncomfortable it would be afterwards, whenever we met in the halls of this apartment house, to have him walk by me with a curt nod.

But I found myself drawn to him. Besides, I could not spend every evening alone in my apartment, as I had for this first week since I had moved in. Oh, not that my spacious three rooms were unattractive. Quite the contrary. But that was just the trouble. The elegance of its high ceilings, and the way warm light flickered over the white wainscoting when I kindled a fire one unusually cool night, reminded me of a long-ago era, when nearly all marriages lasted until death, and an old brownstone such as this sheltered just one large family, not childless couples and singles leading their separate and often lonely lives.

"Thank you," I said. "I'd like to have dinner with you."

He took me to an Italian restaurant on Third Avenue. Midway through the main course he told me that he had been divorced, and I replied that I had, too. Then, answering his unspoken question, I said that the trouble had been "another woman." That wasn't quite accurate. It had been women, quite a few of them.

He gave me a somewhat more expansive account of his own divorce. His wife, a Barnard College graduate, had gone out to California for a summer-school course in filmmaking at UCLA. Instead of returning to New York in the fall, she took a job as a film cutter with a small studio.

"She kept wanting me to come out there. Southern California offered excellent opportunities for an architect, she said. And anyway, why should it be my career that dictated where we lived? Why shouldn't it be hers? I suppose she was right about that, but I just couldn't stand the thought of California."

"And so?"

"And so after two years, during the course of which we'd been together for a total of twenty-three days, we decided to call it quits."

"And you've never regretted it?"

"Never," he said emphatically. He looked at my plate. "Dessert? No? Well, there's this place on Eighty-fourth Street that has a good Dixieland combo."

We left the Eighty-fourth Street place before midnight. On our way home in a taxi, he put his arm around me and said, "Still plenty of time for a nightcap."

He smiled at me. With his sort of hair, dark brown, flecked with gray at the temples, one might expect his eyes to be brown also. But they are blue, with wrinkles at the corners that come from squinting at light on tennis courts and beaches and ski slopes, and also, I suppose, from being past thirty. When he smiles, the wrinkles deepen.

He said, "Your place or mine?"

My stomach tightened. "Neither."

His smile held. "Too soon?"

"No, it's not that."

I looked at the back of the driver's head. Like nearly all New York cabs these days, this one was equipped with a thick plastic pane between the front and back seats, so that a passenger could not press a gun muzzle to the cabby's neck. The pane also makes it difficult for the driver to hear backseat conversations.

I said, "It's just that I'm not interested in casual affairs."

"How do you know it would be casual?"

"Wouldn't it be?"

After a moment he said, "Probably. All right, so what are you interested in?"

"Marriage."

His gaze sharpened. "For someone who went through a divorce court only a few months back, you say that with surprising firmness. Now why do you want to be married?"

"Because I want children. And I believe children should be raised by a couple, not a single adult."

I had been in the care of a couple only for the first two years of my life. Shortly after my second birthday my parents had been divorced and my father, a mechanical engineer, had gone to Arizona, where he soon remarried. When I was four my mother died, and I went to live with my Aunt Gertrude in Albany, New York. She was a good woman, and despite a severe handicap—she was almost totally deaf—she did her best for me. But I always felt that the loneliness of my early years, spent in the silent house of a woman with whom it was almost impossible to communicate, had resulted in a weakness in the very foundation of my life. Perhaps if I had been raised in a more normal home I would not have married a self-indulgent charmer like Gary. Or, having married him, perhaps I would have been strong enough and clever enough to keep him from wandering.

David asked, "Why didn't you have children while you were married?"

"My husband didn't want them."

He asked, after a moment, "Still in love with him?"

"No." Foolish as I had been to marry my husband, I was not foolish enough to go on leaning against that lamppost, so to speak, moaning that he was my ma-a-an, after he'd proved half a dozen times that he could be almost any woman's man.

David squeezed my shoulder and then took his arm away. "All right, so we don't go to bed. But I'd still like to go on seeing you."

I said, pleased and surprised, "Why?"

"The usual reasons. I like to look at you and talk with you. And in your case there's another reason. You're honest. Another girl with marriage in mind might have kept quiet, biding her time. You came right out with it."

We did see each other often, all the rest of that winter. We went to plays and movies, traveled to Stowe twice for skiing weekends, and several times had dinner in my apartment. I knew that he dated other girls and sometimes brought them home to that apartment directly above mine. But in my case the closest he came to lovemaking was the bestowal of a friendly good-night kiss.

In the spring I gradually became aware of a growing inner strain, a sense of inadequacy in every department of my life. Two books I had sponsored vigorously, prevailing over the doubts of associates, turned out to be duds. My employers were nice about it, but I knew that from then on they would place less faith in my judgment. Then, in late April, my Aunt Gertrude died. Standing at the graveside in the Albany churchyard, where patches of snow lingered between the headstones, I realized that except for my father I was alone in the world. And I hadn't seen even him for the past five years. Bound for a job with an Iranian oil company, he and his wife had stopped briefly in New York before flying to Tehran.

True, David stood with me beside Aunt Gertrude's grave that chill afternoon, but I found his presence only a bittersweet comfort. In fact, having him near me often gave me as much pain as pleasure, because by that time, six months after we had met in the brownstone's laundry room, I was in love with him. Obviously he did not love me. I was his friend downstairs, someone he saw between dates with girls who did not have marriage as a goal or, if they did, were canny enough to hide it.

Several times, in desperation, I thought of throwing myself into his arms. But even though I'd proved to be no great judge of men, I was convinced that David was a decent man, far too decent to bed down with me, a marriage-minded girl he had no intention of marrying. If I flung myself at him, he would be disconcerted and guilty. I could imagine him patting my cheek and telling me, like the man in Kipling's poem, that he wouldn't do such because he liked me too much. After that, sheer embarrassment would make us try to avoid each other.

And so I went on, as I had all winter, spending some evenings with David, and far more alone in my apartment. Often as I sat reading in my living room I would hear a girl's light voice and David's familiar deep one in the hall or on the staircase leading upward. Then footsteps overhead and the sound of his stereo, almost inaudible through the thick old floor. Then silence. I would sit there, book forgotten in my lap, fingernails biting into my palms as I stared at the wall, seeing not it but the entwined figures in my far too graphic imagination.

In May all the stresses in my life—lingering self-doubt from my broken marriage, my sense of aloneness in the world, and my hopeless love for David—became too much for me. Even though I'd had symptoms of an incipient crisis, such as sleeplessness and a feeling of nameless anxiety, it seemed to me that my breakdown came with stunning suddenness.

That unseasonably warm morning I emerged from the subway and walked two blocks to Madison Avenue. I felt dizzy and was aware that my heartbeats were both rapid and weak. I turned onto Madison.

And suddenly I was blind. I could hear traffic, voices, footsteps, and the distant wail of sirens. But I could see nothing.

Heart hammering with terror, I leaned against the wall of a building. Even though at that moment I couldn't see it, I knew from all the times I had passed it that it was of polished granite. I could feel the cool smoothness of the stone through the thin white blouse I wore. After a few seconds a woman's voice said, "Are you all right? Can I help you?"

I managed to say, "It's some sort of dizzy spell. Would you walk with me to the Deering Building? It's about the middle of the block."

As I moved forward with my rescuer's hand on my arm, my vision cleared sufficiently so that I could see her, a middle-aged woman, thin and well dressed, with a Saks Fifth Avenue shopping bag in her left hand. At the entrnace to the Deering Building I thanked her, assured her I was all right, and walked across the pink marble floor to the bank of elevators.

My vision was normal now. But as I looked at an elevator's closed bronze door, terror again engulfed me. Terror of the elevator itself, like an upended coffin. Terror at the thought of entering that eleventh-floor office with its book-lined reception room, its big inner room with rows of desks under incandescent lights, its faces that would turn toward me. Over the four years I had worked at Palmer and Company, most of those faces had become familiar to me. And yet now it seemed to me that this morning I would see hostile mockery in them, mockery of me as a woman who could manage neither her career nor her relationships with men.

I turned and fled. At that hour cabs bound for uptown were plentiful. It took me only a minute or so to flag one down.

That evening as I sat in my living room, with the lamp still unlit and the last of the spring daylight pressing against the window, the telephone rang. I looked at it with dread. Someone from my office? After I returned to my apartment that morning, damp with anxious sweat, I had called the office to say that I had a throat infection and could scarcely talk. Was one of my colleagues calling me now, hoping to catch me in a lie? After a moment I forced myself to pick up the phone.

It was David calling. "There are two Garbo films showing at the Thalia. Like to go?"

"I can't."

After a moment he said, "What is it, Diana?"

"I can't."

My repetition of those two syllables must have conveyed my wretchedness because he said, "Whatever it is, just sit tight. I'll be right down."

I got up, unlocked and unchained my apartment door, and returned to the sofa. When David came in I said, "Don't turn on the light."

"All right." He crossed the room, sat beside me on the sofa, and put his arm around my shoulders. "What is it?"

I told him. The attack of hysterical blindness—even then, I was sure it was that, and not a precursor of real blindness—and my senseless terror in the building's foyer, then the taxi ride to this apartment, where I'd sat, numb with fear, all the rest of the day.

"All right," he said finally. He stood up. "Now I am going to turn on the light."

"Why?"

He moved across the room to my desk in the far corner. "Because I'm going to look up your doctor's number and call him." He turned on the desk lamp and picked up the red-leather telephone book, with my name stamped on its cover in gold, which he had given me the previous Christmas. "What's his name? Gorman?"

"Yes. But how can he help me? He's a general practitioner." I heard my voice grow high and thin. "And what's wrong with me is in my head."

"Wherever it is, it can be treated. And if Gorman doesn't know how, he'll know someone who does. I'm going to ask him to see you first thing in the morning." He laid down the book, pulled the phone toward him, and dialed.

Since then I've often wondered about that phone call. Supposing some sixth sense had told me that it would lead me to that turn-of-the-century house, with its battered nineteen-thirties and forties furniture, and its shadowy trio who, if they were real at all, existed on some plane outside of time. Would I still have allowed him to make that call? Sometimes I think I would have.

Chapter 2

The next afternoon, upon the advice of Dr. Gorman, I checked into the Courtney-Latham Clinic.

Courtney-Latham was a relentlessly cheerful place. The staff, even to the elevator operators, kept smiling. Chintz-covered furniture and matching draperies made the rooms look like those of some homey New England inn. The halls were hung with sunny landscapes, and on the long, glassed-in porch overlooking the East River, glazed bowls held the brightest of late spring flowers —lilacs, scarlet tulips, and yellow and orchid irises.

Only the patients were sad. Perhaps on that tall building's other floors, where the truly demented were housed, men and women beamed with the happy confidence that they were the soon-to-be-restored rulers of Russia or of some planet in a far galaxy. But on my floor the patients all looked the way I felt— depressed, anxious, and incapable of ruling even their own lives, let alone Russia.

On my first morning at the clinic I was sent from my own room down to a second-floor ward for a thorough physical examination. The next day and the day after that I spent several hours in the fifth-floor office of a Dr. Winestaff, looking at ink blots, taking word-association tests, and talking of my childhood in that almost always silent house with my Aunt Gertrude. I talked also of my broken marriage and even of my feeling for David Corway.

"You won't tell him, will you, Doctor?" David had visited me twice already, and during the second visit, according to Dr. Winestaff himself, he and David had chatted in the hall.

"No," he said, smiling, "of course I won't tell him."

When he came to my room two afternoons later, Dr. Winestaff suggested that we go out onto the glassed-in porch to talk. There, within sight of the Williamsburg Bridge, and with the hoots of tugs and barges rising from the river below, Dr. Winestaff told me that in his opinion there was nothing seriously wrong with me, either physically or mentally. "But even a structurally sound engine can break down if it is overloaded. What you need is a period of complete rest. Now can you afford to take a leave of absence from your job?"

"I suppose so." Aunt Gertrude's estate had been modest but, such as it was, it had been left entirely to me. I added anxiously, "But if Palmer and Company give me a leave of absence, maybe they won't take me back."

"Miss Garson, I am afraid you exaggerate the extent to which you have fallen down in your work. You must realize that you have a tendency to regard yourself as inadequate, whether you are or not. And even if by some chance your company does not take you back, is that as important as your health? After all, there are other jobs."

"I suppose that's true."

"Now I'm not suggesting a trip to London or Paris. I think you should spend two or three months in some quiet spot, somewhere near the sea, or in mountain or desert country if you prefer."

"No, I like the sea."

"Good." He glanced down at a paper affixed to a clipboard in his lap. "I see that you're to be with us four more days. Perhaps during that time your friend Mr. Corway can find some sort of place for you near the sea."

David did. The afternoon before I was to be discharged, he sat beside me on a wicker settee out on that long porch above the river. "How'd you like to rent a house near Quogsett for the summer?"

Quogsett, I knew, was a tiny village out in the fashionable and expensive Hamptons. "I don't think I can afford anything like that."

"This place is dirt cheap compared to other rentals on eastern Long Island. Forty-five-hundred dollars from now until Labor Day. Of course, it's nothing fancy. Just a frame house built around nineteen-oh-two, or thereabouts. But the location is great. It's just behind the dunes and only a few yards from the beach."

I considered. Even after paying my hideously high bill here at the clinic, I would still have a nice little sum left in the bank. And although forty-five-hundred dollars seemed a lot to pay for about twelve weeks' occupancy of a house, if those weeks restored me to health the money would have been well spent. Besides, I had visited the Hamptons several times, both before and after my divorce, and I loved that part of Long Island.

I asked, "How did you learn of this house?"

"A gal I've known for years has a real-estate agency in Quogsett. I called her up last night. She told me that she's managed the summer rental of this particular house for a number of years. She also said that she'd been holding it for a family who rented it several seasons ago and said they might want it again. But I persuaded her that you needed it more."

What had he told her about me? That I'd had some sort of nervous breakdown, or merely that I'd been ill? And how old was this "gal," and how was it that he could persuade her to rent the house to someone she'd never even met? I looked at him sitting beside me. The rough, dark-brown hair. The squarish face, already tanned although the summer really hadn't started yet. The direct blue eyes and strong nose and humorous, well-cut mouth with its full underlip. It was easy to understand how he had persuaded her, this woman he had known "for years." Probably she had been in love with him all that time.

"What's this real-estate agent's name?"

"Beth. Beth Warren. Diana, you really should rent this house. It's completely furnished, even to linens and blankets. All you'd need to do would be to pack a bag tomorrow and drive out there."

I made up my mind. "I'll take it."

"Good. Now you'll need a car. The nearest grocery store is in Quogsett, more than a mile from the house. Shall I rent a car for you this afternoon or tomorrow morning?"

I nodded. "Make it the cheapest kind."

"Right. You're checking out of here at noon tomorrow, aren't you?" Smiling, he got to his feet. "I'll see you then."

That night, because I feared that the prospect of driving more than a hundred miles to a strange house the next day might keep me awake, I asked the nurse for a sleeping pill. Around nine o'clock I swallowed the yellow capsule. Then, leaving the door open—a rule at the clinic was that patients' doors must be left open at all times—I went to bed and turned out the light.

I don't know when it was that I woke up, aware that someone else was in the room, someone who wept softly and piteously. I sat up in bed. By the dim nightlight from the hall I could see a dark-clad figure huddled on the floor a few feet away from the bed, head and crossed arms resting on updrawn knees, long hair hiding the face.

I said, "Who are you? What are you doing in my room?"

A low voice, hoarse with weeping, said, "I gave away this little dog of mine. She loved me so. Twice she ran away and came back to me, and each time I called up her new owner to come and get her. Oh, it was such a wicked, wicked thing I did, such a wicked thing."

"Please," I said. "Please go back to your own room. Shall I ring for the nurse so she can help you?"

"No! No nurse." She stood up, her face a vague white blur in its frame of dark hair, and silently walked out of the room. I turned over in bed and, after a while, slid back into sleep.

At the moment that nighttime visit had not struck me as strange. But the next morning it did, chillingly so. Disturbed patients, I'd been told, were treated on other wards. It seemed highly improbable that anyone on my floor would invade a stranger's room to sob out a confession about a dog. In fact, it seemed so improbable that, sickeningly, I began to doubt that it had happened.

There was nothing "seriously wrong" with me, Dr. Winestaff had said. But doctors, like everyone else, sometimes make mistakes.

It wasn't until one of the day nurses had finished helping me pack my suitcase that I summoned up enough courage to mention the weeping woman. "One of the other patients came into my room last night. I woke up and saw her sitting on the floor, crying. She said it was over a dog she'd given away."

Before she veiled it, I caught an odd expression in the nurse's eyes. Then she smiled. "You must have had an exceptionally vivid dream, Miss Garson. No one on this floor would behave like that."

Because I was frightened, I spoke more forcibly than I would have otherwise. "It was not a dream! She was here. There wasn't enough light for me to see her face clearly, but she had long dark hair, and she was small, only a little over five feet, I'd say, and I got the impression that she was around thirty years old."

"There's no patient of that description on this floor." Then she added quickly, "But perhaps there was last night. A few times, since I've been here, there has been a mixup, and newly admitted patients have spent a few hours on the wrong floor before the mistake was discovered. Maybe that happened last night, and the patient was reassigned to the proper ward before I came on duty this morning." She paused. "Shall I try to find out if something like that happened?"

I looked at my watch. A quarter of twelve. Probably David already was in the downstairs office where I was to sign out. I didn't want to keep him waiting. Besides, I thought, feeling a chill ripple down my spine, what if the nurse learned that there had been no misassignment, no woman of the sort I had described wandering around this ward the night before? Better just to assume that there had been. Better just to try to forget it.

"Thank you," I said, "but it doesn't really matter."

By three o'clock that afternoon, when with David at the wheel of a rented green VW we drove east on Long Island's parkways, I had managed to forget the weeping woman. One reason was that I found it wonderful to sit beside David in the little car, with our shoulders sometimes touching when we rounded a curve. For another, it was a perfect early June day, with a few fluffy clouds sailing across the blue, and the roadside trees still clothed in the pale green of newly unfurled leaves.

After a while the heavy traffic of Queens and Nassau counties thinned out. By the time we reached the Hamptons the roads were even less crowded. We bypassed Southampton, drove along Bridgehampton's quiet main street, with its one-story shops and high-steepled churches, and then took a route leading across level fields white with potato blossoms. Soon we were driving down Quogsett's main street, past scattered houses set far back from the road, past a one-room schoolhouse painted a bright red, and past a one-story building, straight out of Norman Rockwell, which housed the post office and general store. According to white raised letters on one of its plate-glass windows, it also housed the Warren Realty Agency. We parked the VW behind a bright-red Datsun and went inside.

The woman who rose from behind a desk was somewhere in her middle thirties, model thin and model tall, as tall as David, in fact. She wore a cashmere sweater almost the same shade as her curly red-brown hair, a brown and red plaid skirt, and high-heeled brown leather boots. During our drive from New York, David had told me that he'd met Beth on a summer vacation several years before, that as far as he knew she had never been married, and that she'd lived on eastern Long Island since childhood. "But she's no bucolic spinster type. You'll see."

I certainly did see. Obviously Beth Warren bought her clothes, if not in Bloomingdale's or Bergdorf's, then in Southampton's smartest shops. Something else was obvious, too, from the way she looked at David and from her courteous but constrained manner toward me when he introduced us. She and David had been lovers once. Recently? I did not think so. But however long ago it had been, she had not forgotten, even if David might have.

She said, "We'd better take my car, too. I'll lead the way."

The three of us went out into the late-afternoon sunlight. Following Beth Warren's red Datsun, we turned left off Main Street and then left again along a narrow road paralleling potato fields and, beyond the fields, a line of dunes. Soon we turned off onto a dirt road, little more than two car tracks, that led toward the ocean. The road ended between two tall dunes. The Datsun stopped, and we stopped behind it. To our right, facing the road, stood a weathered brown frame house with a somewhat dingy white trim. From its second-floor windows, obviously, one could see over the dunes to the beach.

Beth Warren walked back to us, twirling a key ring around a slender finger. "Here are the keys to the front and back doors. Do you mind looking at the house by yourself? I want a chance to go over the list of houses I'm to show after dinner."

I said, taking the keys, "You mean you are showing properties at night?"

"Yes. This is my busiest time, just before the season starts."

David said to me, "I'd better go in with you, just in case you come across a stuck door or something."

Perhaps Beth had hoped that she and David might share a few reminiscences while I inspected the house, but if so her manner did not betray it. She said, "I'll be waiting in my car."

David and I walked up broad wooden steps that could have used a coat of paint. I reflected—correctly, as I later learned—that this house must have been built by a farmer. That was why it sat sensibly behind a sheltering dune instead of perched atop it, in easy reach of summer hurricanes and winter gales. That was why it faced the road and the potato fields beyond. If he chose, the farmer could take his ease on the veranda once in a while and still keep an eye on his hired hands.

David unlocked the golden-oak front door and we went inside. I liked the house immediately. Oh, not that it appeared in any way distinguished. The hall, papered in a faded yellow floral pattern and carpeted with a worn brown runner, stretched back to a steep staircase, also carpeted in brown. A few feet before one reached the foot of the stairs, a wide doorway opened into the living room. It was a room that would cause any decorator to shudder. Wicker chairs and settees mingled with sagging upholstered pieces. There was an upright piano with yellowed keys, a tall console phonograph of the sort you seldom see except in an antique shop, and a golden-oak bookcase. Through its glass doors I could see worn copies of long-ago best-sellers I'd always planned to read—*The Sheik*, for instance, and *A Girl of the Limberlost*.

David looked around him, grinning. "Beach house art nouveau," he said. "But then, what can you expect for forty-five-hundred dollars?"

"I like it," I said, and I did. For one thing, evidently one of those Hampton groups or individuals who ready houses for summer occupancy had been at work here recently, because I caught the scent of lemon furniture polish and of floor wax. What was more, the atmosphere seemed to me friendly and homelike, almost as if the house were welcoming me. That, I realized, was a strange notion. Over the years dozens of different summer tenants must have sat in those wicker chairs and picked out tunes with one finger on those yellowed piano keys. The atmosphere should have been almost as impersonal as that of a motel room, but it wasn't.

We walked back through the adjoining dining room—round golden-oak table and octagonal chandelier with a shade of milky green glass—to the kitchen. It seemed adequate, even though the gas range was old and cheap, the sinkboard cracked, and much of the silverware in a cabinet drawer either rusted or bent out of shape.

We climbed to the second floor. Just as I had guessed, from the windows of the largest bedroom one could look out over the dune to the wide beach and the Atlantic beyond. Even though the season had not started yet, there were a few people out there enjoying the late afternoon sunlight. A wader-clad fisherman, waist-deep in water, was surf casting. A young man and woman, both in khaki shorts and white T-shirts, moved slowly over the sand, each grasping a hand of the plump toddler who walked between them.

Next to the big bedroom was a bathroom with a claw-footed tub and with a floor covered with green linoleum. Across the hall were two smaller bedrooms. David said, looking in at one of the rooms, "I hope you plan to ask me frequently for the weekend."

My pulses quickened, but I managed to keep my voice light. "Any time."

"Great. But as I told you on the way out, it can't be for a while. We're going to be busy as hell for at least ten days with specifications for that Universal Towers Building. In fact, I'd better take the train back to town tonight."

I felt a pang of disappointment. I had hoped that in spite of job pressures he would stay over until the next day. "Well, if you must."

We walked to the end of the hall and then through an unlocked door to a kind of second-floor gallery or narrow porch that ran clear across the rear of the house. Leaning against the wooden railing, I looked down at a tangle of eel grass, wild pink roses, and wild sweet peas of various colors that stretched between the house and a one-car garage with a few missing roof shingles. Directly below where I stood was a shallow basin of cracked cement, about eight feet in diameter. Eel grass and other vegetation grew in the cracks. "I wonder what that was," I said.

"Lily pond? Wading pool? Whatever it is, it hasn't been used for a long time. Well, do you like the house?"

"I love it!"

Again following the Datsun, we drove through near-sunset light back to Beth Warren's office. There I signed the lease and made out a check and handed it to her.

"Thank you, Miss Garson. Now about the phone in that house. Shall I have them send someone to connect it for you?"

"Please do."

"If you have any complaints about the house, or any questions, please feel free to come to me at any time."

"Thank you. Come to think of it, I have one question right now. What is that cement basin behind the house?"

"As I understand it, many years ago it was a pool for Mrs. Woodhull's children. That was when they were small, of course. She didn't want them going unaccompanied down to the beach."

"Mrs. Woodhull?"

"The Woodhull family used to live there part of the year. The house was built by her father, a potato farmer. He left the house to her. By that time she'd married a wealthy Southampton man, but she kept that house behind the dune because she liked to stay there with her two children during the summertime."

"Does Mrs. Woodhull still own the house?"

"No. She and her children—only they were no longer children by then—were killed in a boating accident about twenty-five years ago. Mrs. Woodhull's sister, a Miss Gowrey, owns the house now."

"And lives there in the wintertime?"

"No, Doris Gowrey has a small house in East Hampton. She says that she can't live right beside the ocean because of her rheumatism." She glanced at her watch. "Now, if you want to buy groceries, Miss Garson, the store next door will remain open for about half an hour. Starting the first of June, they stay open until seven-thirty."

David said, looking at his own watch, "Good lord! I'd better get to the station or I'll miss my train back to New York."

"All right," I said. "I'll take you there."

"No, you'd better get your groceries before the store closes. Beth, would it be too much trouble—"

"Of course not. I'm going home for a while anyway, and the Bridgehampton station is only a few miles out of my way."

I said good-bye to them outside the office, and then moved slowly toward the grocery store next door. On its steps I paused to look after the red Datsun driving away down the wide street, now barred with the long shadows of the elm trees that lined one curb. Before they went to the station, would they find time for a drink somewhere? Well, what difference if they did? I tried to shove the thought aside, but it still hovered at the back of my mind while the grocer and his wife, at my direction, packed cans and cartons and netted bags of vegetables into a cardboard box.

Soon after I entered the house beside the dune, though, I no longer thought of David and Beth. A strange contentment wrapped me. I prepared my dinner—a hamburger patty and onion rings and a lettuce-and-tomato salad—placed the thick crockery plate on a battered blue metal tray I'd found in the kitchen cabinet, and carried the tray out to the porch. Seated in a wicker chair drawn up to a rickety wooden table, I ate my meal and, just as the farmer father of that woman—what was her name? Woodhull?—must have done long ago, I looked across the dirt road to the potato fields, their blossoms a white blur in the gathering dark. As I rinsed the plate and battered silver afterwards, I was pleasantly aware that if I chose I could climb the dune and sit there for half an hour or so, watching the stars come out and the last glimmer of light fade from the sea. But I didn't choose to. I'd had a long day and I was tired, contentedly tired. By the time I had unpacked my bag in the big bedroom and made up my bed with sheets and blankets from the linen closet I'd seen in the upstairs hall, I would be ready for sleep.

Sometime during the night the sound of soft laughter and murmuring voices woke me. The sound seemed to come from inside the house. I lay there in the darkness, not in the least frightened, just puzzled. The sound *couldn't* be inside the house. For one thing, I'd locked both front and back doors before climbing the stairs. For another, people who invade a darkened house at night don't advertise their presence with talk and laughter, however subdued.

I got out of bed, walked to the window, and looked out over the dune at a stretch of beach and ocean. A last-quarter moon was up now. Shining through a horizon mist, it cast a faint orange light on the wave-fringed water and the sand. The beach appeared entirely empty.

Then something to my left down on the beach caught my eye, a reddish glow. I leaned farther out the window. Someone had built a fire on the beach and left the embers still alive.

So that was it. A couple, or perhaps several people, had spent the evening around a beach fire. Then, just minutes ago, they had passed this house on the way to their car, parked somewhere up the road. It must have been their talk and laughter that I heard.

The night had turned damp and cool. I closed the window. Still with that contentment, that sense of being at home in this house, even though I had never seen it until today, I turned and went back to bed.

Chapter 3

Some hours later I awoke to gray light, and to rain striking the windows with a sound like that of flung pebbles. So that horizon mist last night had been a harbinger of a change in the weather. Well, it didn't matter that I could not start on my tan today. There would be many, many days for lolling on the beach. Today I would explore this house.

After a leisurely breakfast, which I ate in solitary state in the dining room rather than in the kitchen, I went into the living room and opened the glass-fronted bookcase. Seated on the straw rug, I read several pages at random in *The Sheik,* and then turned to *A Girl of the Limberlost.* Gene Stratton Porter, I found, brought to moths and butterflies almost the same panting interest that Edith Maude Hull felt for her lustful hero. I put the books back in the case and then opened the doors of the cabinet phonograph. Dozens of records stood on edge in the vertically divided compartments. I lifted the stacks out, placed them on the floor, and went through them.

Over the years, many temporary tenants must have left records here when they returned to the city. If these recordings had ever been sorted out as to era or type of music, they were certainly in no order at all now. A Mick Jagger LP, for instance, was sandwiched in between worn and visibly cracked recordings by Caruso and Harry Lauder. But most of the records were from the Big Band era of the thirties, forties, and early fifties. Feeling an odd excitement, I realized that when those records were bought this house was not available to any summer tenant who had the price. A family had lived here in the summer in those days, Mrs. Woodhull and her children.

And what of Mr. Woodhull, the wealthy Southamptonite that she, a farmer's daughter, had married? Had he, too, left some mansion on Gin Lane or First Neck Lane each year to live in this house during the summer months? I had an impression that Beth Warren had said that only Mrs. Woodhull and the children had spent summers here.

I played some of the records on the old phonograph. "Dockman and Roe at the Palace," a recording of a long-ago vaudeville sketch filled with jokes so witless that they seemed to me, paradoxically, downright hilarious. "Indian Love Call," recorded by Jeanette MacDonald and Nelson Eddy. And Jan Garber's "Harbor Lights," an old standard, melodic and wistful, which in my mind was vaguely associated with World War Two or perhaps the later war in Korea. "Harbor Lights" was still revolving on the turntable when I heard a car stop outside. Looking through the front window, I saw it was a phone company truck.

Once the telephone man had hooked up the phone and left the house, I climbed to the second floor. At the rear end of the hall was a steep flight of wooden steps, little more than a ladder, leading up to a trap door. I climbed the steps, seized the door's metal handle, and pushed upward. The door's hinges, I found, held it open in an upright position, rather than allowing it to slam back against the attic floor. Prepared to retreat if I found the attic too dark or dusty, I poked my head through the opening.

Obviously, whoever had been hired by Beth Warren to ready the house for summer tenants had worked up here, too. Rainy gray light came unimpeded through well-washed windows at either end of the attic. No cobwebs hung from the rafters, which met in a V overhead. And although the attic harbored furniture even more worn than that in the living room, all of the pieces— the backless kitchen chair with peeling red paint, the blue plush sofa with springs resting on the floor, the bookcase with one door missing and the glass of the other jaggedly broken—were arrayed in a neat line on the attic's left-hand side. I climbed the rest of the way through the opening, went straight to the bookcase, and gingerly opened that broken glass door.

Here was reading matter too dull to appeal to even the most bored summer tenant: *The American Horse Doctor, The Potato Growers Manual for 1908, Everywoman's Guide to Tatting.*

But underneath a stack of old *Popular Mechanics* was a flat, wide volume with dark-red covers. Again with that odd little leap of excitement, I recognized it as a photograph album. I laid it on the attic floor and opened it.

Inside the front cover were the words, "Property of Grace Woodhull," written in a small feminine hand. The pages of black paper that followed were filled with snapshots, each with a caption beneath it, written in white ink and in that same feminine hand. The photograph in the top left-hand corner of the first page showed three people standing on the porch of this frame house, smiling at the camera. The figure in the middle was a slender woman of forty-odd, with either brown or dark-blond hair. On her right stood a dark-haired, handsome youth of about twenty. On her left was an extremely pretty blond girl of perhaps sixteen. The woman wore a blouse and skirt. Both the younger people were in dark jerseys and white duck trousers. The caption read: "June 2, 1948. Derek, Sheila, and I. The Woodhulls return to the old place, not just for summer but for good."

Which was the "I" of the snapshot? The woman? Almost certainly. And who had taken the picture? The next snapshot and caption answered both questions. It showed the boy and girl, still in the same clothes, but this time flanking a thin black woman in a maid's uniform of some light-colored material. The caption read: "Also on moving-in day, Derek, Loretta, and Sheila."

The Woodhull family album. Or perhaps more accurately, the last or one of the last of their albums. There must have been earlier ones, holding pictures of Derek and Sheila when they were young children, young enough to splash about in that long-unused pool behind the house.

The light would be better down in the living room. Still with that strange sense of eagerness, I picked up the album and descended those steep steps, pulling the attic door closed after me. When I reached the living room I sat down on the straw rug and slowly turned the album's pages.

Scores of snapshots, each with its dated caption, spanning the years from 1948 to 1953. Pictures of Sheila, long legged in very short shorts, holding the handlebars of a bicycle. Of Mrs. Woodhull standing beside a shiny sedan. (Beneath it she had written: "My brand-new 1951 Studebaker and I.") A smiling Derek in swim trunks, looking bronzed and even more handsome than in earlier snapshots, holding a surfboard poised above his head. Photographs of beach parties—and of Christmas trees of various years, standing in one corner of this now-silent room where I sat on the floor. A color snapshot of Sheila in a backless sundress of some green material. She sat on the bench of that upright piano over there, smiling over her shoulder. The color photograph showed just how pretty she had been, with light golden hair, blue eyes, and warm skin tones. Another photograph, also in color, showed her seated with updrawn knees on a sand dune. Beside her sat a dark, intense-looking young man, identified in the caption as "Win Chalmers." His arm was around her shoulders, and he was looking, not at the camera but at her. Strange, but just by looking at a snapshot made more than a quarter of a century ago, I knew how fiercely and possessively he had loved her.

The last two pages of the album—or rather, the last two that held pictures—were given over mainly to photographs of Derek Woodhull. A close-up of Derek at the wheel of a powerboat. The caption read: "Derek aboard his twenty-third birthday present from his father." Longer shots of Derek standing at the boat's rail showed that it was a cabin cruiser of perhaps twenty-five feet. A shot of the stern showed that the boat had been named the *Wave Dancer*.

Below the row of boat pictures there was a snapshot of handsome, smiling Derek in an army uniform, with a lieutenant's bars on his shoulders. Underneath the picture, the now-familiar handwriting had been not quite steady: "My son, Derek Ainsworth

Woodhull, off to war. September 15, 1952." The rest of the page was covered with snapshots Derek must have mailed home from Korea, pictures of himself and of various uniformed companions against bleak backgrounds of treeless hills and plains.

On the next page were the three final pictures, all of them color snapshots. One showed Sheila, in a strapless blue evening gown, seated on the piano bench. Beside her stood Derek, still in uniform, but now with a captain's bars on his shoulders. The other showed Derek and his ecstatically smiling mother seated on a high-backed Victorian sofa that even though it no longer stood in this room, looked familiar to me because it was part of so many of the album's snapshots. Beneath both pictures Mrs. Woodhull had written in a larger than usual hand, "Home safely at last, thank God! May 18, 1953."

The last photograph showed Derek and Sheila smiling down from the rail of the *Wave Dancer*. To Sheila's left, and standing well apart from her, was a child, a tall, thin girl of not more than twelve and possibly as young as ten. There was something familiar about that square, unsmiling face. Something sad and withdrawn, too, as if more than two feet of space separated her from the smiling, handsome young Woodhulls. The caption read: "Derek and Sheila and Elizabeth Bratianu."

I turned the last page. No more photographs, but a newspaper clipping had been affixed to the page with transparent tape. According to what Mrs. Woodhull had written at the top of the clipping, it was from the East Hampton *Star*'s June 4 edition. The headline read: "War Hero Returns to Hamptons."

My eyes skimmed down the column. Captain Derek Woodhull, decorated Korean war veteran, had been honored at a dinner that past week by the Merchants' Club of the Hamptons. A second Korean veteran, Lieutenant Larry Philbeam, had also been honored at the dinner.

"Captain Woodhull's father, Mr. Gregory Woodhull of Southampton," the last paragraph read, "is a well-known real estate developer."

I read the item through again. Lieutenant Larry Philbeam. Even though I didn't bother to check it right then, it seemed to me that the captions of two or three of the Korean snapshots had listed a Larry Philbeam.

I frowned at the last paragraph. Gregory Woodhull, husband of Grace, father of Derek and Sheila. No pictures of him in this album, and only one mention of him, in the caption under the photograph of Derek at the wheel of the *Wave Dancer*. Obviously the Woodhulls had been separated. In fact, they must have been separated before the first of these snapshots was made, since its caption referred to Mrs. Woodhull and her children returning to "the old place, not just for the summer, but for good."

But even though he lived apart from his family, Gregory Woodhull apparently had continued to provide well for them. They'd had at least part-time domestic help, good clothes, and good cars. And then there was that expensive cabin cruiser—

Hadn't Beth said that the Woodhulls had died in a boating accident? Was it the *Wave Dancer* that had carried them to their deaths?

Beth, short for Elizabeth. I turned back to that last photograph. Yes, the chic and attractive Beth Warren, twenty-five years ago, might have been that thin, gloomy-looking child. But, if so, how was it that she, who had never married, should now have the last name of Warren? Perhaps she had changed it by some other means.

Yesterday she had handed me the keys to this house, saying that if I didn't mind, she would remain in her car to go over a list of rental properties. At the time, I had considered her excuse valid. But now I wondered if it was some childhood memory of the Woodhulls, or a knowledge of something that had happened in this house, that made her want to enter it as seldom as possible.

Beth had said that if there was any way she could be of service, she hoped that I would call her. Well, I did have a legitimate question or two—how to dispose of trash, for instance, and was there a beach where I might dig clams? I would telephone her tomorrow and suggest that we have lunch together.

I found that my pulses were racing at the thought of questioning her about the Woodhulls. Fleetingly, I realized that this was very unlike me. Most of my adult life I had been too taken up with my own problems to feel undue curiosity about others. But now something—perhaps something in the very atmosphere of this house?—had made me feel an almost-compulsive need to learn more about the people who had lived here, and who had died their violent deaths while I was still an infant in arms.

I became aware that the light in the room had brightened. Looking out through the front window, I saw a patch of blue sky with ragged clouds fleeing across it. Absorbed by the album, I hadn't even noticed that the rain had ceased. I glanced at my watch. How had it gotten to be seven o'clock? After placing the album atop the bookcase, I went back to the kitchen.

As I ate my dinner in the dining room, with frozen broccoli accompanying the rest of the hamburger, I wondered how it was that the album had been placed up there in the attic for any summer tenant to leaf through. Even if it was only some hired person who had gone through the possessions in this house after the Woodhulls' deaths, surely that person had told Gregory Woodhull of the album's existence. No matter how bitter his relations with his wife, surely he would have wanted an album containing some of the last, if not the very last, pictures taken of his son and daughter.

And if for some inexplicable reason he had come to regard his own offspring with indifference or aversion, that still left the present owner of the house, Mrs. Woodhull's sister. Why hadn't she claimed this memento of her sister and her niece and nephew?

For the first time I realized that, just as Derek and Sheila's father was absent from those snapshots, so was their aunt. And that seemed strange, since according to Beth Warren, the woman lived only a few miles away, in East Hampton.

After dinner I carried an old sweater up to the dune's top and spread it out on sand still damp from the rain. The ocean and even the deserted beach reflected the pastels of the sunset sky, soft pink and pale gold. Gradually the colors faded. The ocean became a tranquil gray and then darkened as the last of the light drained from the sky. I stayed up there on the dune until the moonless sky was strewn thickly with stars. Then, with sand sliding from beneath my feet as I descended the dune, I went back to the house.

More than once during the night I awoke with a sense that I had heard—in a dream or half-waking—voices and the sound of movement through the house. Each time, somehow not in the least frightened, I went back to sleep.

Chapter 4

The next morning was bright but cool, with a salty breeze ballooning the white dining room curtain inward while I ate my breakfast of scrambled eggs and toast. After I'd washed the plates I'd used, I went to the telephone, looked up Beth Warren's office number, and dialed.

She accepted my luncheon invitation promptly. In fact, I got the impression she had her own curiosity to satisfy, most probably a curiosity about David and me. She said, "I have business in Southampton this morning. Would you mind meeting me there someplace?"

"Not at all." Southampton was only about ten miles away, and on this sparkling day it would be a pleasure to drive along the Hamptons' tree-bordered roads.

"There's a small restaurant on Job's Lane called The Road Race. It has excellent food."

"That sounds fine. Will about one o'clock suit you? . . . Good. I'll be there."

After I'd hung up, I turned back to the phone book. Since I was going to Southampton anyway, I might as well drive past Gregory Woodhull's house, if he still lived there.

There was no listing for a Gregory Woodhull. Perhaps his number was private. Perhaps he no longer lived in Southampton, or anywhere else. Then I remembered that there had been a blue-covered *Social Directory of the Hamptons,* issued only two years before, in the bookcase. I opened one of its glass doors and took out the directory.

At least up until two years ago, a Gregory Woodhull had lived with his wife Caroline (nee Tate) on First Neck Lane, Southampton.

A few minutes before one I drove down curving Job's Lane, Southampton's smart shopping street. Some of the stores, offering dresses or sporting goods or fine porcelain and silver, were open. Others were still closed, awaiting the traditional June 15 opening date. Near the foot of the street I saw a one-story frame structure with a painted sign, The Road Race, above its doors. I parked a few feet farther on and walked back.

The restaurant was indeed small, a single long room with booths along one wall and a counter along the other, its stools occupied by well-dressed men and women, most of them young or youngish. Some, I realized, must be proprietors of nearby shops. Others, in shorts or slacks topped by sweaters, had the look of summer people who hadn't waited for the season to start before they opened their houses. Both side walls of the restaurant were covered with photographs of racing cars and their helmeted drivers. As I stood hesitating in the doorway, Beth Warren leaned out of one of the booths and beckoned to me, smiling.

"Good to see you again, Miss Garson," she said when I sat down on the bench opposite her. "Or would it be all right to call you Diana? After all, we have a friend in common."

"Diana will do fine."

"Good. And I'm Beth." She handed me one of the two menus lying at the table's edge. "I can recommend the spaghetti with pesto sauce."

We both ordered the spaghetti. While we waited for our food, I asked her about the trash. "I've been putting it in that rusty old wire incinerator behind the house, but I haven't lighted it. The wire is broken in places. I was afraid burning fragments might escape."

"Good thing you didn't light it. It's all right to store your trash in the incinerator, but don't burn it there. That's against the law. Take it to the dump."

She told me how to find the dump. Then I asked her about clamming.

"There are places to clam all around the shores of Peconic Bay. One of the best places, though, is the beach near Southampton College. But you'll need a permit. You can get it free of charge at the town hall in Southampton."

The waiter brought our spaghetti. It was very good indeed, and I told Beth so. "Yes," she said, "all the food here is good. In fact, this is my fiancé's favorite restaurant."

"You're engaged?" I looked at the diamond solitaire on her left hand. "Stupid of me, but I didn't notice your ring the day before yesterday."

"I wasn't wearing it then. I'd taken it to the jeweler's because the setting was loose." She paused. "Have you known David long?"

"Only since last October."

"I met him five years ago, right after his divorce." Her smile was wry. "Attractive, isn't he?"

I nodded. "But elusive."

"That depends upon what you're trying to catch him for," she said dryly. "If it's just for bed, he's quite available. But if you hope to marry him, the way I hoped to catch him on the rebound after his divorce—" With a shrug, she stopped speaking.

"Well, everything turned out all right. You're engaged to someone else."

Her voice still held that dryness. "And darned lucky to be. He's a highly successful businessman, the owner of the General Motors franchise out here on the East End, with headquarters in Southampton and showrooms in several other villages. And I—well, I'm a single gal of almost thirty-seven."

"But you're a very attractive woman!"

"Thanks, but I still think I'm darned lucky."

We ate in silence for perhaps a minute. Then I asked, "Did you know that the Woodhulls' family album is in that house I rented? I found it up in the attic."

After a moment she said, "No, I didn't know. I've scarcely been in the house since I started handling its rental. There's no need for me to be. A local cleaning agency gets the house ready in the spring, checks it for damages before the tenants leave in the fall, and then cleans it again."

"To judge by the pictures in the album, Mrs. Woodhull and her son and daughter were all very good-looking."

"Yes, I believe they were."

"Believe? I thought that when you were a child you might have known them. I mean, David said you'd grown up out here. And besides, there was a girl of about ten or eleven in one of the album snapshots. Mrs. Woodhull's caption said the little girl's name was Elizabeth, and she did look the way I imagine you may have at that age. The last name, though, wasn't Warren. It was some sort of middle European name."

Beth had been looking down at her plate. Now she raised her head and her red-brown eyes looked straight into mine. "The name was Roumanian. Bratianu. It was my mother's name. I never knew what my father's name was. I doubt that my mother knew, either."

I said, appalled, "Oh, please! I didn't mean to—"

"It's all right. Almost any old resident out here could tell you my history, and might do so. My mother—she worked as a clerk in various New York department stores—died when I was nine, and the court assigned me to a children's home in Rockland County. About a year later an East Hampton couple named Warren, a doctor and his wife, took me to live with them for the summer. The idea was that if they still liked me in the fall, they might adopt me."

"And that's how you met Grace Woodhull and her children?"

"Yes, the Warrens and Grace Woodhull were friends. In July of that year the Warrens decided to go to a medical convention in London and then stay on over there for a few weeks. The Woodhulls offered to let me stay with them while the Warrens were away. Derek Woodhull was home from Korea by then, and so I shared a room with Sheila." She paused. "The only time I can remember that I had my picture taken with any of the Woodhulls was over at the Sag Harbor marina. Mrs. Woodhull stood down on the dock and took a picture of Derek and Sheila and me standing at the rail of Derek's boat."

I felt ashamed of myself. I'd always felt a certain amount of self-pity because of my parents' divorce, and my mother's death, and the subsequent years spent in Aunt Gertrude's too-silent house. But at least I had known the identity of the man who fathered me. And I had always known that I was loved and wanted, first by my mother and then by my aunt. I thought of the child Elizabeth in that old snapshot. No wonder that, expressing in body language the sense of the gulf between herself and the handsome, happy Woodhulls, she had stood well apart from them at the cruiser's rail. And no wonder that the small, square face had looked bleak. After all, she hadn't even been sure whether in the fall she would be adopted by the Warrens or returned to the children's home.

I asked, "Was that the boat on which the Woodhulls died?"

"The *Wave Dancer?* Yes. The Woodhulls had taken her up to Maine that September. They were on their way home when the boat caught fire one night a few miles off the Massachusetts coast. A Coast Guard patrol saw the flames, but before they could reach the *Wave Dancer* the fuel tanks exploded. Bits of floating wreckage were found, but the bodies were never recovered."

I shivered. "Good thing you weren't aboard the *Wave Dancer* that time."

"Yes, a good thing."

"And the Warrens did adopt you?"

She nodded. "Dr. Warren has been dead for several years. Mrs. Warren—I call her Aunt Eunice—has been in a nursing home in Queens for the past three years. I go to see her regularly, but it's rather pointless. She seldom knows me."

I said awkwardly, "I'm sorry that your parents—I mean, your adoptive parents—"

"I know. But I had them both for quite a few years, long enough to grow up, and pass my state realty board examination, and open my agency."

"Do you like the real estate business?"

"Love it. Of course, I don't like showing the Woodhull house. It's not that I was so terribly fond of them. I was such an uptight little kid, afraid to love anybody lest I immediately lose them. But they were kind to me, especially Mrs. Woodhull, and I hate to be reminded of what happened to them." She looked at my empty plate. "Have you room for dessert? The zabaglioni is awfully good here."

"Then let's have some," I said, and changed the subject, asking her about restaurants and night spots I remembered from my several brief visits to the Hamptons.

We had almost finished dessert when a man of about fifty, dapper in charcoal-gray slacks and a blue sports jacket, stopped beside our table. In contrast to his gray hair, his thin face was deeply tanned. He said, "Hello, Beth. I saw your car across the street, so I figured you were in here."

"Hello, Win. Darling, this is Miss Garson. Diana, this is my fiancé, Winstead Chalmers."

Winstead Chalmers. Win Chalmers. Wasn't that a name from one of those captions in Mrs. Woodhull's album? If so, the man standing here now almost certainly had been in one of those old snapshots. It was unlikely that, among eastern Long Island's sparse population, there would be two men with such a distinctive name.

I murmured an acknowledgment. The smile he gave me was pleasant but impersonal. I reflected that even though he was years older than she, Beth was lucky in her "highly successful" fiancé in more ways than one. Obviously he was the sort who concentrates on one woman, or at least one woman at a time.

Beth said, "Will you join us, Win?"

"No, thanks. I just dropped in to say hello. See you tonight. Nice to have met you, Miss Garson."

When he had gone, I said, "You must have known him for years."

"That's right. But how did you know?"

"His picture is in the Woodhull album."

She looked puzzled for a moment and then said, "Oh, I know how that came to be. Win was engaged for a short time to Sheila Woodhull. Of course, that was before the Warrens brought me to the Hamptons from that children's home. Still, I have a dim recollection of seeing him around that summer. Not that I really noticed him, anymore than he noticed me. I was a child then, and he was just another grown-up, twenty-two or some such advanced age."

Now I realized which of the photographs he had been in. The one of him and Sheila seated atop a sand dune. I recalled the intensity in his thin young face as he looked at her. Easy to guess that it was Sheila, not the youth who adored her, who had broken the engagement. I tried to imagine what a young man capable of such intensity must have felt when he found himself discarded. Hatred? Almost surely, at least for a while.

Beth wanted to pay the check, but I reminded her that it was at my suggestion we had lunched together. We parted out in the cool, bright sunshine, she crossing the street to her Datsun and I walking a few yards to my VW.

When I was behind the wheel I hesitated. Return to my temporary home? No, since I was already in Southampton, why not take a look at Gregory Woodhull's house? I was curious about it, this house that Grace Woodhull had left to live with her son and daughter in the farmhouse her father had built. I thought I knew where First Neck Lane was. If I remembered correctly, it was the first turn to the left after you passed the movie theater on Hill Street.

A few minutes later I was driving down a wide, quiet street. Through gateways set in tall hedges and brick walls I could see the spacious houses of the rich, many of them a gleaming white and ornamented with turn-of-the-century cupolas. There seemed to be no street numbers, only the names of residents on small signs set near the curb or affixed to gateposts.

There it was, the name Woodhull on a gray fieldstone gatepost set in a ten-foot-high yew hedge. The gate stood open, affording me a glimpse of the sprawling house, also built of fieldstone.

I drove past and then angled the little car into the curb and stopped. My pulses were rapid. I could drive in there and try to see him. I had a more or less legitimate excuse. And again, I was feeling that compulsion, so much stronger than simple curiosity, to learn more about three people who, one night a quarter of a century ago, had vanished beneath the black Atlantic. I backed up a few yards and turned in between the gateposts.

The drive was a circular one, looping past stone steps that led up to tall, grille-protected glass doors. I stopped at the foot of the steps and sat there for a moment, mustering up my courage and rehearsing what I would say to the butler or maid who opened the door. Then I got out of the car.

At that moment a man appeared around the corner of the house, an old man in a wheelchair. He stopped for a moment and then continued toward me, gnarled hands propelling the wheels.

When he was only a few feet away he stopped again. His still-thick hair was white. His face, strong of nose and square of jaw—the sort of face you see again and again in the pages of *Fortune* magazine or on museum busts of Roman senators—was deeply lined, and his mouth drooped a little on the right side. His eyes, though, gray beneath dark eyebrows, were fierce and bright.

He said, "Who are you?" His legs, in flannel trousers, were very thin, I noticed, but the shoulders stretching his red sweater were those of a once-powerful man. "What do you want?"

Disconcerted by his abruptness and his bright stare, I said, "I hoped I might see Mr. Gregory Woodhull."

"I'm Gregory Woodhull."

I was startled. Somehow I had thought of him as being about the same age as Grace Woodhull in those snapshots. I hadn't taken into account that twenty-five years had passed since those pictures were taken, nor that she probably had been at least a few years her husband's junior.

"My name is Diana Garson," I went on nervously. "I've rented the house that your wife—I mean, your late wife—"

I broke off. He said coldly, "And so?"

"I ran across something I thought you might want. It's Mrs. Woodhull's photograph album. It has snapshots of her and of your son and daughter in it."

His face flushed. He said, in a thickened voice, "I had no son and daughter."

Bewildered, I looked at him. Why should he deny parentage of his children? Had a stroke addled his wits? Or had something happened before their deaths, something that had embittered him to the point that he repudiated even their memory? It was hard, at least, to imagine him turning that much against his son, his handsome son to whom he'd given a cabin cruiser as a birthday present. But evidently Gregory Woodhull was that bitter.

Before I could think of anything to say, two women came around the corner of the house. One was tall and thin and dark and wore the white uniform of a nurse. The other looked as if she had stepped out of a photograph in a chic magazine devoted to country living. Pale blond hair drawn back into a knot. Pink cotton shirt with its sleeves rolled up, and full pink and white checked skirt. Rawhide sandals on slender tanned feet. In the basket she carried over one arm I could see several longstemmed roses and the handles of a pair of garden shears.

Stopping, she gave me a cool little smile and said, "Yes?"

Now that she was close I saw that she was older than I had thought at first, probably in her late forties. I said, "I'm sorry. I'm afraid I've intruded."

"You have," Gregory Woodhull said.

"Greg!" She put her hand on his shoulder. "Why don't you let Miss Coswell take you back to the rose garden, where you'll be sheltered from this breeze? It's far too cool for you out here."

"All right, Caroline. But get rid of her." He didn't look at me as the nurse, grasping the chair's handlebar, turned it round and wheeled it toward the corner of the house. Face burning, I got into my car.

The blond woman hurried toward me. "If my husband was rude, you must forgive him. He is not well." Her voice was pleasant but her blue eyes were appraising and wary. "Now what is it you wanted?"

I gave her my name, and explained about the album. "I thought he might want it."

"Quite a natural assumption. But there is something you couldn't know about. My husband's relations with his first wife were far from—cordial."

"But even so," I blurted out, "I should think he would want pictures of his children!"

The blue eyes became quite cold. "I'm afraid, Miss Garson, that my husband's attitude toward those two is a matter we don't discuss." Her tone added, "with outsiders."

She stepped back from the car. I managed to frame some sort

of farewell. With my stomach a tight knot of humiliation, I circled around the drive and returned to First Neck Lane. Obviously both Gregory and Caroline Woodhull considered me an insensitive busybody. And perhaps today I had behaved like one. What was wrong with me? As I have said, in the past I had always been too taken up with my own problems to take an undue interest in the lives of others.

As I turned off First Neck Lane onto busier Hill Street, I resolved to forget about Grace and Derek and Sheila Woodhull. Why should I keep thinking about people I had never met, people who had died twenty-five years ago? From now on I would follow the prescription Dr. Winestaff had given me at the clinic. I'd swim, dig clams, lie in the sun, and just relax.

Despite that resolve I still had a sense of humiliation as I applied for my clam-digging permit at the town hall, bought a large supply of groceries at the Southampton supermarket, and drove toward Quogsett. But almost as soon as I unlocked the door and stepped inside the house, a grocery-filled bag in each arm, the tension began to drain from me. I felt secure and at peace with the world, almost as if this house, its furniture scarred by the occupancy of dozens of casual tenants, was, in fact, still the home of one happy family, a family of which I was a part.

After my solitary meal I again left the house, this time to walk along the sunset-dyed beach with a half-dozen long-legged sandpipers skittering ahead of me, racing after each wave as it withdrew and then retreating as the next wave advanced. When it began to grow dark I returned to the house. I opened the bookcase, took out a copy of *Old Wives' Tale*, and read for about an hour, enjoying the novel far more than I had when I read it in high school. At last, pleasantly sleepy, I went up to bed.

Sometime in the night the sound of a piano awakened me. After a moment I recognized the tune. It was "I'll See You Again," from some Noel Coward musical.

Not thinking at all, and with a strange stilling of all my senses, I got out of bed. I didn't stop to put on slippers or a robe. Out in the hall I switched on the overhead light. Halfway down the stairs I halted.

From there I could see part of the living room, dimly illuminated by the hall light. A girl sat at the piano, a girl in a strapless blue evening dress, smooth bare shoulders gleaming faintly in the uncertain light. She was leaning forward so that her blond hair, almost shoulder length and curved under at the ends, hid her profile.

Then she turned her face and smiled at me. She was Sheila Woodhull.

And then she was gone. One instant she was there, smiling that friendly smile. The next she was not. There was only the empty piano bench and the piano itself, standing silent.

I thought then, Am I mad? Truly mad? In spite of what Dr. Winestaff had said, was I mad even before I left the clinic?

On the other hand, perhaps that figure I had just seen down there in the living room had an existence outside my mind, an existence of its own.

I became aware of a chill feeling down my spine and along my arms and legs. With a strange detachment I realized that my body was reacting with fear to whatever it was that had been down there on the piano bench. It was as if my body perceived a danger that my mind did not. In fact, my thoughts were quite calm. If I was mad, then I was mad. And if phantoms moved through this house—well, it would be hard to fear a phantom whose smile was friendly, almost loving.

Not forgetting to turn off the hall light, I went back to bed.

Chapter 5

When I awoke the next morning I lay quietly for a time, thinking, what a strangely vivid dream. And it had been strange, too, in that part of the time, I had seemed to stand outside my own dream, wondering if what I saw as I stood on the stairs was in some way real or just a hallucination.

But there was nothing strange or hard to understand about the origin of my dream. I had seen several snapshots of Sheila Woodhull seated at the piano, and in one color photograph she had been wearing a strapless blue evening dress. It was also easy to understand why my unconscious mind had chosen that particular song for the dream-Sheila to play. When I went through the records in the old phonograph cabinet I had noticed a single of "I'll See You Again." I recalled thinking at the time that probably that record had been bought by the Woodhulls, rather than by anyone who had occupied this house in more recent years.

Again, just as in my dream, I felt that chill rippling of the skin, which, I had heard, was a reaction inherited from our half-animal ancestors of millions of years ago, whose hackles rose when danger threatened. And yet there had been nothing threatening in the dream. Quite to the contrary. It had been pleasant to have the dream-Sheila look up at me with that friendly, almost loving smile, as if she were the sister I had never had.

In addition to that strange mingling of uneasiness and pleasure, the dream had left me with something else, a renewed urge to learn more about those three people and their violent deaths. Gone was my resolution of the day before to forget about the Woodhulls. Oh, I still regretted my visit to Gregory Woodhull. But surely there was no reason why I should not look up matters that were part of the public record.

After breakfast that morning—another beautiful morning, and warmer than the day before—I spent about two hours doing accumulated housework, sweeping, dusting, and carrying out to the incinerator the trash I would later cart to the dump. Then I packed myself a lunch—two ham sandwiches and an orange. After that I changed into a swimsuit plus white shorts and a T-shirt, went out to the garage, and took the clam rake down from its hook on the wall.

A few minutes later, as I drove down the narrow side road toward the wider one paralleling the shore, I wondered where I should go first—to the newspaper office in East Hampton, or to that clamming beach near Southampton College. Aware of a driving need, I decided upon the East Hampton *Star's* office.

The main street of East Hampton, uncrowded on this early June day, stretched wide and beautiful, with the narrow pond that divides it for part of its length reflecting giant elms and the façades of gracious old houses. I found a parking place only a few feet from the *Star's* entrance. A pleasant young woman in the paper's front office assigned me to a small table near the window and then brought me a bound volume containing editions of the month and year I had requested.

It took me only a few minutes to find the story. The front page headline read: "Three Presumed Lost in Explosion at Sea." My eye hurried down the first paragraph:

> Mrs. Grace Woodhull, 46, of Quogsett, and her son Derek, 26, and daughter Sheila, 21, are presumed dead in the fire and explosion last Friday night of the power cruiser, *Wave Dancer,* off the Massachusetts coast. A fourth passenger, Elizabeth Bratianu, 10, was found by Coast Guardsmen floating in a lifebelt in the water and was taken to Boston's Grimshaw Memorial

Hospital, where she is still being treated for burns and exposure.

Rigid with surprise, I stared down at the newsprint. Yesterday I had said to Beth, "Good thing you weren't aboard the *Wave Dancer* that time," and she had replied, "Yes, a good thing." Why had she allowed me to believe something that wasn't true? I looked down at the paper and went on reading:

> According to a Coast Guard spokesman, the child at first told a confused story about a masked person boarding the *Wave Dancer* from a smaller boat, ordering her to put on a life jacket, and then tossing her overboard. According to the child's story, as relayed to the *Star* by the Coast Guard spokesman, a few minutes after she landed in the water she heard shots aboard the *Wave Dancer*, followed by the flickering light of flames. Then she saw the smaller boat pulling away from the power cruiser. After that, when she had drifted some distance from the *Wave Dancer*, she saw the boat explode. The spokesman says the Coast Guard doubted the girl's story. Just before press time, a telephone call from the *Star* to Grimshaw Memorial Hospital elicited the information that the child now seemed to have no memory whatever of the fire or explosion, or of how it came about that she was floating in the water.

The rest of the story followed the lines of what Beth had told me the day before. The Coast Guard patrol had spotted the *Wave Dancer* fire from several miles off. Before they could reach the stricken vessel, it exploded. Because the continental shelf at that point is scored by a number of deep fissures, it was probable that the bodies would never be recovered. The story's last paragraph read:

> The only immediate survivors are Gregory Woodhull of Southampton, husband of Grace Woodhull and father of Derek and Sheila, and Miss Doris Gowrey of East Hampton, Mrs. Woodhull's sister. Mr. Woodhull gave his son the power cruiser as a twenty-third-birth-

day present. Later Derek Woodhull served with the infantry in Korea, where he was decorated for bravery and promoted to a captaincy. He had been out of the army only a few months when the tragedy occurred.

So, I thought fleetingly, the Woodhulls had been only separated, not divorced, at the time of Grace Woodhull's death. Why hadn't they made the break between them official? Had Grace Woodhull refused to give her husband a divorce?

My thoughts returned to Beth Warren. Strange that she should have told her rescuers that story about a masked someone boarding the power boat. But then, children's imaginations, especially if stimulated by something they had seen on TV or in the movies, could be both powerful and grotesque.

I returned the volume to the pleasant woman who had brought it to me, thanked her, and left.

I found that the day had grown even warmer. As I drove along Montauk Highway, my delight in the hot sunlight striking through the car's window to lie on my arm and the sight of the fields and the old farmhouses with rainbow-hued iris beds on their front lawns made the Woodhulls fade to the back of my mind. When a sign, "Southampton College, next left," loomed up, I slowed for the turn, bumped over the railroad track, and passed the lawns and red brick buildings of the college campus. A few minutes later, after driving along a series of streets bordered by summer cottages, many of them still shuttered, I drove onto a spit of gravelly land projecting into the bay. With delight I saw that there was only one vehicle there before me, a red pickup truck. I could see its probable owner wielding his clam rake out in the water, far beyond the seaweed-and-shell-covered flats now revealed by the low tide. In the dazzling sunlight his head and upper torso, all that was visible of him, looked black against the blue water.

Hungry now, I ate my lunch sitting on a towel spread out beside the VW. Then, not wanting to go into waist-deep water too soon after I had eaten, I put on sneakers and waded, crunching, across the layers of empty mussel shells, with rubbery amber seaweed waving around my legs, and schools of tiny fish fleeing ahead of me. When it seemed to me that about an hour had passed, I returned to the VW, stripped down to my swimsuit, applied sunburn lotion, and then, carrying the clam rake and with my rubberized beach bag slung from my shoulder, moved out into the water. It was cold at first, but my body soon became used to it.

My luck was not phenomenal. Most of the time the contents of the heavy clam rake I laboriously lifted to the water's surface were rocks, together with clams less than the legal one inch in length. Occasionally, though, the rake held a clam I could keep, its ridged shell shading from gray to dark blue, and the feel of it pleasantly cool and heavy in my hand. I forced myself to stop when I'd dug up half a dozen. They would make an ample chowder-for-one tonight. And I had best not try to store uncooked clams, not in that antediluvian refrigerator with no freezing compartment.

When I returned to the car and took my watch from its glove compartment I saw with surprise that it was almost four. I drove home, pleasantly tired, pleasantly aware of my sun-warmed, salt-encrusted skin. As I neared the shabby house beside the dune, my sense of contentment increased.

I drove into the garage, restored the clam rake to its wall hook, and then, carrying my bag of clams, entered the house by the back door. After rinsing the clams at the sink, I put them in the refrigerator. I was on my way to the foot of the stairs, intending to take a shower in that claw-footed tub, when the phone rang in the living room. I went to it.

"Diana? This is Beth Warren."

I sensed that she had tried to speak pleasantly. A certain sharpness came through, though. "Hello, Beth."

"Would you let me buy you a drink this afternoon?"

"You mean right away? I've been clamming, and I was about to take a shower."

"There's no great rush. Would an hour from now give you time enough?"

"I think so."

"I thought we could meet at Bobby Van's in Bridgehampton. Do you know where that is?"

"Yes." I also knew that the café had a clientele that ranged from local fishermen and farmers to various literary figures who had retreated more or less permanently from Manhattan to the fields and beaches of the Hamptons.

"See you there in an hour, then. I'll be sitting at the back."

Because of the tension in her voice, I asked, "Did you want to see me about something special?"

"Yes. Special to me, anyway." Before I could speak again, she hung up.

An hour later, wearing blue jeans and a lighter blue T-shirt, I walked from the still-bright sunlight of Bridgehampton's main street into the café's cool interior. At the near end of the bar, gaze fixed broodingly on the glass in his hand, sat a famous playwright whose dramas both intrigued and bewildered me. At the far end, each holding a beer glass, stood a group of broad-shouldered, jovial-faced men who, from the snatch of conversation I heard as I passed them, were lobster fishermen. The prize-winning playwright and the lobstermen seemed equally at home.

I moved toward the shadowy back region of the long room. At this in-between hour most of the tables there were empty. Beth waved to me from a table against the wall. As I approached her I saw that she was wearing a long-sleeved beige silk shirt and a beige and brown plaid skirt, and that she looked every bit as chic as she had the two previous times I had seen her.

We spoke of random matters—the playwright at the bar, the beauty of the day, my so-so luck at clamming—until the waiter brought us our white wine and returned to the front of the room. Then Beth said, "I hear you visited the East Hampton *Star* today."

"Why, yes. But how—"

"The woman who runs the general store next to my office told me. You bought groceries from her, remember? She happened to be in East Hampton today, and saw you coming out of the *Star* office. When I went into her store this afternoon to buy some nail polish—mine had chipped—she mentioned seeing you." She laughed, not very pleasantly. "Don't look so surprised. This is a small community. Why, in all of the Hamptons there are no more permanent residents than in a few square blocks in some

parts of Manhattan. And so everybody knows what everybody
else does, and talks about it."

The covert hostility in her manner was awakening hostility in
me. "And so I was seen coming out of the *Star* office. What
about it?" I asked, although I was already sure of the answer.

"I know a woman who works there. She said you'd wanted to
look up something in a back number of the paper. Because of
the month and year you asked for, I knew what you were interested in."

She no longer tried to hide her unfriendliness. "Why were you
checking up on what I told you yesterday? Why are you so interested in people you never knew, people who died before you
were born, or almost before?"

I said haltingly, "I'm not sure why. Perhaps it's because I
found that album."

"At least a few other summer tenants must have gone up into
the attic, on a rainy day, let's say, and looked through that old
album. But that didn't launch them upon a career of digging up
information about the Woodhulls. Not one of them even mentioned the album to me, let alone invited me to lunch so they
could ask questions about it. That was why you asked me to
lunch, wasn't it?"

"Partly," I admitted.

"And now you feel you've caught me in a lie. Well, I didn't
tell you that the Woodhulls had taken me with them on that
cruise to Maine because I don't like to talk about it. I don't like
even to think about what happened to them, or to me, either.
Here, let me show you something."

She undid the smart gold link that held her left cuff in place
and rolled up her sleeve. A wide scar ran from her wrist almost
to her elbow. "I have another scar on my left shoulder. They
gave me skin grafts, and the grafts took all right, except that the
burned area stays white if I try to tan, and looks awful. That's
why I wear long sleeves, both winter and summer."

I said, "I'm sorry. It must have been very painful and frighten-
ing, especially for a child."

"Believe me, it was." She paused and then said, "That bit in
the *Star* about my telling the Coast Guardsmen that someone

had come aboard the *Wave Dancer* from another boat. I don't remember telling anyone anything like that. In fact, when I woke up in the hospital the next day all I could remember was going to bed in the smallest cabin in the cruiser and then finding myself floating in the water. It had seemed to me I was miles from the burning boat, although I suppose it was only a few yards. Then there was a terribly loud noise, and pieces of flaming wood or something fell from the sky. Then, after what seemed a long time, a man was carrying me up the side of another boat, the Coast Guard boat."

After a moment I said again, "I'm sorry. And I'm sorry I've made you feel you had to talk about this."

"Well, you couldn't know how I felt. But I still don't understand why you became so interested in the Woodhulls in the first place."

I said slowly, "As I told you, there was the album. And also—"

I hesitated, reluctant to ask a questioin that would be so self-revealing. Yet I needed very much to know the answer.

I said, "Do you know if any other people who rented that house found anything—strange in the atmosphere?"

The red-brown eyes regarded me for a long moment. "Strange? What do you mean?"

"A kind of—sense of movement through the house. Sounds. And maybe even actual—"

I broke off. She said, "Do you mean *ghosts?*" Her mouth twitched at the corners, but I had a fleeting sense that she was not as amused as she appeared to be. "Impossible! Why, that house is about as ordinary as they come. In all the years I've been agent for the place I've never had a tenant complain of any sound stranger than a dripping faucet or a window frame rattling in the wind.

"Of course," she went on deliberately, "I've heard that people who believe in such things feel that a recent illness may—what's the word? Oh, yes—may sensitize a person, lay them open to—psychic influences. Perhaps that's supposed to be especially true if the person's had some sort of nervous disorder."

Nervous disorder. Had David told her that I had spent a week at the Courtney-Latham Clinic? He might have. Eager to obtain for me the rest and quiet Dr. Winestaff had prescribed, David might well have said, "This girl's had sort of a nervous breakdown, Beth, so I figure she needs that house more than those other people you had in mind."

David. Strange to think that, though I loved him, I hadn't thought of him even once during the past forty-eight hours.

Beth leaned toward me. "Diana, if you have—feelings about that house, you shouldn't stay there. I can still rent it to the people I originally intended to have it this summer. And I know of a sweet little cottage just off Main Street in East Hampton. It's close to everything—the movies, the shops, Guild Hall, the library, everything."

I stiffened. "No!" The house was mine. I'd paid the whole summer's rent in advance, and it was mine.

"But, Diana, if you have uneasy feelings about that house, and if they are going to cause this—this rather morbid interest of yours in something that happened twenty-five years ago—"

Translation: If you're going to keep on rummaging around in something that is none of your business . . .

When I remained silent, she went on, "Because I'm engaged, I don't want anyone stirring up talk about things that happened away back then, things that people have more or less forgotten. Oh, Win knows all about me—that I was illegitimate, that I got these scars in that boating accident, and so on. But he doesn't like to think about it. He's a conservative businessman, with a big social and economic stake in the community. I'm sure he'd much prefer that I had been born into one of the old families out here, and never suffered anything more traumatic than having to wear braces on my teeth, and never had my name in the paper except in the social news. Yes, that's the sort of woman he wishes he were in love with."

I said, remembering the possessive way he had looked down at her in that restaurant the day before, "But he is in love with you."

"Yes, intensely so. Win is a very intense man, and always has been. But that is precisely what worries me. If people start talking about the days when I was not Beth Warren, but a skinny orphan with a funny-sounding foreign name she'd gotten, not from her father—whoever he was—but from her mother— Well, Win might react just as intensely against the idea of marrying me."

How sad, I thought. How sad to fear repudiation from a man for something that was no fault of hers. I said, "I didn't mean to stir up talk."

"I know you didn't. And if you'll just forget about the Wood-hulls and what happened to them—well, everything will be fine."

A subtle threat there, a threat that otherwise she might find some way to evict me from the house. "All right," I said.

She smiled at me and then glanced at her watch. "I'd better get home. Win is taking me to dinner at eight."

"Where is home?"

"I have one of the few apartments in East Hampton. It's on the upper floor of an old house on Main Street."

We walked out past the long bar. The lobstermen must have gone home to supper, but the playwright was still there, and still staring down into his glass.

Out on the sidewalk, in the reddening light of a sun near the horizon, Beth and I said good-bye. Our farewells were polite, but the mutual hostility was there, just below the surface. Neither of us mentioned seeing the other again.

As I drove toward Quogsett, I reflected that I really shouldn't feel hostile toward her. Naturally she was anxious not to lose the wealthy man who had asked her to marry him.

Still, I had this indefinable but distinct impression that she had more reason than Winstead Chalmers' probable displeasure for not wanting anyone to stir around in the past. What precisely *had* happened off the Massachusetts coast that night twenty-five years before? I thought of the terrified child babbling to her rescuers about someone boarding the *Wave Dancer—*

It would not be such a fantastic-sounding story now, in the last quarter of the twentieth century, when many pleasure boats in Caribbean waters have been boarded by modern pirates, criminals who kill the passengers, toss their bodies overboard, and then sail to Central American ports, where men in the drug trade buy the stolen boats. But back in those days there was no flourishing drug trade, and consequently no great demand for stolen boats. Besides, the *Wave Dancer* had not been stolen. It had been destroyed by fire and an explosion. No wonder the authorities had doubted the hysterical child's story, even before she herself had contradicted it by saying she had no memory of her last hours aboard the cruiser.

But what if her first story had been the true one? What if, even today, she was concealing a memory of some figure stepping silently over the *Wave Dancer*'s rail?

I thrust the thought aside. There was no point in asking myself a question to which I could never know the answer. Besides, I was nearing the house, standing shabby and yet somehow very dear at the end of the rutted road, and already I felt that sense of warm content stealing over me.

I put the VW in the garage and entered the house by the back door. I walked along the hall to the living room, now filled with evening shadows, and took *Grand Hotel* from the glass-fronted bookcase. Late as the hour was, I felt determined to have my clam chowder. I would read in the kitchen while the mixture of chopped clams, onions, and potatoes simmered on the stove.

By the time both the clams and the vegetables were fork tender, I had read a third of the way through Vicki Baum's novel of Berlin in the nineteen-twenties. On a battered tray I carried the book and the bowl of steaming chowder into the dining room and placed them on the golden oak table beneath the glass-shaded chandelier. For about twenty minutes I divided my attention between the book and the chowder. Perhaps because I myself had lifted those clams from their bed of sand and gravel, I found it the best chowder I had ever tasted.

It was past eight-thirty by my watch now. Sunburned and slightly stiff from my clam-digging, I was beginning to feel sleepy. I left the book on the table so that I could resume reading while I ate breakfast, took the tray back to the kitchen, and washed the soup bowl and spoon I'd used. Then I walked back along the hall through the lingering June twilight toward the foot of the stairs. I'd already put my hand on the newel post when, for some reason I cannot name, I turned and looked through the wide archway into the living room.

A slender woman stood at one of the windows, her back toward me.

Slowly I moved to the threshold. Grace Woodhull turned from the window and smiled.

"Come in, Diana."

Chapter 6

Although aware of the prickling of my skin, I moved with a dreamlike calm into the room. Grace Woodhull's plain dark shirtdress was familiar to me. She was wearing it in a number of those old snapshots.

She said, "We wanted you to know how happy we are to have you here."

We? Still with that dreamlike sense of serenity, I looked to my left. Wearing a blouse and full cotton skirt of some pale color—the light was too dim for me to be sure just what color—Sheila Woodhull sat in one of the old armchairs. Her smooth blond hair shone faintly in the uncertain light. Derek Woodhull, in khaki uniform, stood beside her, one forearm resting on the chair's high back. I could see the gleam of the captain's bars on his shoulders. He was smiling.

I heard my own calm voice. "You are not real, are you?"

It was Derek Woodhull who answered, still smiling. "It depends upon what you mean by real."

I thought about that for a moment. "I mean," I said, "it's only because I am— It's only because I've been ill that I see you."

Grace Woodhull said, "Perhaps that makes it easier. But anyway, we are glad that you see us."

Slowly I turned my head to look at Sheila. She didn't speak, just smiled that friendly smile.

Mrs. Woodhull said, "You look tired, Diana. Perhaps you had best go up to bed."

"Yes," Sheila said, "you do look tired."

"All right." I turned. As I walked toward the hall I was aware of them moving after me to stand grouped at the foot of the stairs. "Good night," the woman said, and Derek and Sheila echoed, "Good night."

Halfway up the stairs I looked back. The hall was empty.

But they had been there. I had seen and talked with them, and I would again.

A voice deep within me said, "You stayed here too long. They have you now."

For a moment I felt a distant terror, like the beating of a far-away drum. Then the feeling faded, and the sense of warm contentment came back.

I climbed the rest of the stairs, went to bed in the big bedroom, and, if I remember correctly, went to sleep immediately.

I did not see them in the morning, a morning of misty sunlight filtering through fog, but I seemed to feel their friendly presence in the house. It was with reluctance that, around eleven in the morning, I realized I would have to go out for groceries. Unwilling to risk another encounter with Beth Warren, I drove, not to the general store in Quogsett, but to an East Hampton supermarket.

By the time I returned to the house the fog had disappeared. Again with that sense of reluctance, I put on a swimsuit and walked past the dune to the beach. After all, if one rented a waterfront house, one should use the beach. It was still quite empty, no swimmers at all—perhaps the water was too cold—and only a few scattered couples and family groups stretched out on the sand. In late afternoon another fogbank formed on the horizon and began rolling shoreward. Glad of the excuse, I picked up my beach towel and hurried back to the house.

Did I see the Woodhulls again that night, or was it not until the next night? I don't know. That whole week has a dreamlike quality in my memory, with no clear demarcation of the days. I know that one night in the lamplit living room—did I turn on the lights, or was it one of them who did?—I danced with Derek to "Harbor Lights," one hand on his shoulder, with its captain's bars, the other clasped by his hand, warm and pleasant feeling to my own. Grace Woodhull and Sheila sat on the sofa, smiling as they watched us.

Then for a bleak moment, the spell seemed to lift. I wondered what someone out there in the dark, looking through a window into this lighted room, would see. A young woman dancing by herself to music audible only to her ears? Briefly I felt cold and lost and terrified. Then, once again, the room was warm and friendly, and the music lovely and wistful, and I could think of no place I would rather be than right here, dancing with this handsome, smiling man while his mother and sister, also smiling, watched us from the sofa.

I said, "Is it because you were wearing a uniform in many of those last snapshots? I mean, is that why I see you this way?"

"It's as good a reason as any, isn't it?"

"I suppose so."

The music ended. I said, "I'd best go to bed now."

"All right, Diana. Good night." And Mrs. Woodhull and Sheila said, "Good night, Diana."

That was the most detailed of such recollections from that week. Most of my memories are fragmentary and almost as brief as those in some movie montage designed to telescope time and space. Looking up from a book to see Mrs. Woodhull seated across the room from me, her smooth dark head also bent over a book. Derek and Sheila seated at the piano, playing a four-handed version of some tune I recognized then but can't identify now. Derek, hand outstretched to me in invitation, while once again the strings and muted brasses of "Harbor Lights" issued from the console phonograph. My most poignant memory, though, is a generalized one, a sense of warmth and safety and of belonging, belonging to a family of pleasant and attractive people. The life I'd known in New York—the breakup of my marriage, my job troubles, my painful love for David—seemed remote and unreal. Rather than the Woodhulls' intruding upon my era, it seemed to me that I had moved back to theirs, a simpler, safer time, when no one had heard of skyjackers, or angel dust, or punk rock, and only one American out of a hundred, say, knew where Vietnam was.

I lived life on another level, too, of course, during that week. I sat on the beach, and shopped for groceries, and cooked them on the gas range. (I never saw the Woodhulls in the kitchen. I don't know why. Could it be because all of the indoor snapshots in that album had been taken in the living room?) I even went clamming again one afternoon, and then hurried back to the house with only about half as many clams as I had planned to dig.

Once more that week the enchantment vanished, leaving me as chilled and bewildered as if a blast of icy wind had struck me. It happened one afternoon in East Hampton. I emerged from the supermarket, put my groceries in the little car's trunk, and then, eager to get back to the house, started driving along the village's broad and gracious main street. I'd driven about half of its length when the cold thought struck me. What had happened to me? Why did I hurry so eagerly toward a house that I knew sheltered no living person but myself?

Was I mad? Could it be as simple as that—if, of course, you could ever call madness simple? Or was it true, as some people believed—among them intelligent and even distinguished people —that the dead could return, even from fathoms deep in the sea?

The library, I thought. Perhaps there were books that could help me.

I parked the car opposite the library in front of Guild Hall, the gracefully sprawling white brick structure that is the center of East Hampton's cultural and entertainment life. As I got out of the car I saw, beside the walk leading to the hall's entrance, a glass case containing a poster. It bore a picture of Dick Cavett, together with the announcement of a Guild Hall play in which he would star. Cavett's face, intelligent and merry and so much a part of the present time, increased my sense that I had been living in a shadow world, perhaps of my own making.

I climbed the steps to the library, an attractive brown-shingled building with ivy-hung walls, and went inside. To the pleasant gray-haired woman behind the desk, I said, "Do you have any books on the occult?"

Even as I said the word I hated it. Occult was a word I associated with women I had glimpsed in New York on upper Broadway, anxious-looking women, usually overweight and with shopping bags in their hands, slipping into doorways to climb steep stairs to second-floor "gypsy tearooms." Those tearooms, I'd heard, were frowzy places where you could drink wretchedly made tea at two dollars a cup and then have a "psychic" read your future in the tea leaves. And now it was I standing here asking for books on the occult.

The librarian looked nonplussed. She said, "Well, I know we have William James's *Varieties of Religious Experience.*"

"I read that in college. It isn't exactly what—"

"Oh, I think I know what you mean." Her smile had brightened. "Books on supernatural phenomena. We have a book called *Haunted Houses,* I know, and perhaps a few others of that sort. I'll consult the card catalogue. Do you have a library card?"

"No."

"Well, you can skim through the books while you're here."

I sat at one of the tables and looked through the four or five volumes she brought to me. None of them was helpful. Accounts of shadowy ladies in gray appearing on the staircases of French chateaus, and riders in the dress of eighteenth-century highwaymen galloping along moonlit English roads, and antebellum Louisiana mansions where, some said, you could hear at night the moans of slaves once imprisoned in the attic by their sadistic mistress. Most of the accounts mentioned a coldness in the air at the time of these phenomena. All of them mentioned the fear, even horror, of those who witnessed such manifestations. None of them seemed to parallel in any way the warm sense of contentment, of *belonging,* that I had felt in that house, and in the presence of those three smiling people from the sea.

I carried the books back to the desk, thanked the librarian, and left.

I did not get into my car. Needing distraction, I walked to the busier part of Main Street, visited an art gallery that offered paintings of Long Island scenes, loitered before shop windows, went into a lunchroom for coffee that I didn't really want. Then I went back to my car.

It was sunset now. On the road between East Hampton and Quogsett the sky's golds and flaming pinks dyed the potato blossoms in the fields and even shimmered softly on the highway itself. By the time I turned onto the road paralleling the dunes, that bewildered, frightened feeling had dropped from me, almost as if it had never been. I felt soothed by the evening's beauty and content to be driving toward the house beside the dune, that oft-rented house that seemed nevertheless to be home, not only to those three others, but to me as well.

Chapter 7

The next morning I had just finished dressing in jeans and a T-shirt when I heard the blast of a car's horn outside. A second later the sound came again, strident, imperious. Puzzled, I moved to the bedroom window and looked out. A well-polished but ancient black sedan stood down there in the narrow dirt road. The driver was a woman. I could see one shoulder and arm, clad to the elbow in a sleeve of green and white print. Again the horn sounded. Then she leaned out of the car with her face turned toward the front door. I saw the glitter of her glasses.

Resentful, I called down, "Just a minute, please," and turned from the window. As I moved along the hall and then down the stairs I was aware that the day, at eight-thirty in the morning, was already hot. Full summer, apparently, had arrived overnight.

I went down the walk and stood beside the car. "Good morning." I saw that she was somewhere past sixty, with coal-black hair that looked undyed even in the bright sunlight, and a thin, deeply lined face. A certain bitter set to her lips made me feel that it was chronic discontent, rather than the years, which had carved those facial lines so deeply.

"Are you Miss Garson?"

"Yes."

"I'm Doris Gowrey, the owner of this house."

Doris Gowrey, Grace Woodhull's sister. "Oh, yes." Despite the antagonism in the gray eyes behind the steel-rimmed glasses, I tried to sound friendly. "Your agent, Miss Warren, mentioned you to me. Won't you come in?"

"What I have to say can be said right here." She added, with obvious reluctance, "Or, if you don't want to go on standing there, you can come around and sit in the car."

"Thank you." My tone was stiff now. I circled the old car's front end and sat down beside her. She was anything but a frail-looking woman, I saw now. Her shoulders were wider than average under the dowdy print dress, and her hands, one on the wheel and the other resting on her thigh, were almost as large as a man's.

"Miss Garson, it wasn't until last night that I knew you were in my house."

My temper rose. I wanted to say, I signed a lease that says that for the next three months it's *my* house. Instead I said nothing.

She went on, "Beth Warren had given me to understand that my house was to be occupied by a family who had rented it twice in the past, but when I phoned Beth just to make sure, she said that she had rented it to a young woman named Diana Garson."

Again I said nothing.

"Now I have a proposition for you," she went on. "I will refund all your money, making no deduction for the time you have already stayed here. Then Beth Warren can find you another place, perhaps more suitable. Smaller, I mean. I'm sure that there are still plenty of summer rentals available."

My resentment boiled over. "I find this one suitable. And anyway, why should you want to refund my money?"

"Because I don't want a single woman, especially a young one, as a tenant! Beth Warren knows that. I understand it was a man who persuaded her to disregard my wishes in this instance. I assume he is someone who was once—a close friend of hers and is now a close friend of yours."

Close friend, I gathered from her tone, was her euphemism for bed partner. I said, feeling my face grow hot, "I know that in the past landlords often discriminated against single women. But that's against the law now."

"Oh, yes! That's the way the law is nowadays. Civil rights for this group and that group and the other. All except the landlords. No one cares about the landlords' rights to do as they want with their own property."

"You have a point there," I admitted. "But in my case you have nothing to worry about. That man friend you mentioned may spend a few weekends here later on. Surely it's my privilege, as the tenant of a three-bedroom house, to have him as my guest. But I won't throw parties, or leave lighted cigarettes on the furniture—I don't even smoke—or in any other way mistreat your house. I like this house, Miss Gowrey. And so even though it is generous of you to offer a refund, I must refuse."

Her eyes seemed to glitter behind her glasses, but otherwise she made no reply. I went on, "Surely, now that you have seen me, you can't object too strongly to my occupying your house. After all, I'm not a giddy teenager. I'm a twenty-six-year-old woman with a responsible job in the city."

She looked at me for a long moment and then burst out, "I can't see why you should want to stay here, considering what you told Beth Warren about my house."

My nerves tightened. "What exactly—"

"You told her you thought there was something strange about the house! Now listen to me, Miss Garson. Offhand I don't know how many tenants, married couples and families, have spent summers in that house since I inherited it. But I do know that not one of them ever found anything in the least peculiar about the place. I need the income from this house, need it to live on. And if you start circulating rumors that the house is haunted—"

"I haven't circulated any rumors! I came out here to *rest*, Miss Gowrey. Why, except for Beth Warren and a few tradespeople, I've scarcely spoken to anyone since I've been here."

It must have been Beth who gave her the idea I might be circulating rumors. Had Beth also somehow learned of my visit to that Southampton mansion on First Neck Lane and passed the information on to Doris Gowrey? If so, Miss Gowrey didn't mention it.

I said, "It was this album I found in the attic that made me curious about—about your sister's tragedy, Miss Gowrey. It's full of pictures of her and of her son and daughter." After a moment I added reluctantly, "I suppose I should turn it over to you."

I waited apprehensively for her answer. I'd been quite sincere in offering the album to Gregory Woodhull. But that had been days and days ago, before my sense of kinship to those three had grown strong.

I needn't have worried. She said deliberately, "For all I care, you can burn it." Then for the first time she gave a small smile, a grim one. "That shocks you, doesn't it, sophisticated big-city girl though you are. Well, let me tell you, Miss Garson, my sister ruined my life."

As I just looked at her, surprised and incredulous, she said, "Yes, ruined it! Everything she had should have been mine, because Gregory Woodhull was mine. I attracted him before Grace did. I was younger than her, and prettier. Oh, don't look at me like that! I know how I look now. But I was pretty then. Grace, though, had this way about her where men were concerned. And when she quarreled with the man she really wanted to marry, and he went away— Well, she looked around to see who else was available, and there was Greg."

She fell silent for a moment and then went on, "She made him miserable, of course, especially after the man she'd really wanted to marry came back to the Hamptons."

"If she really wanted the other man," I said, "then why didn't she try to get a divorce and marry him?"

"Marry Travis Eaton? Because," she said drily, "by then Travis wasn't available. He'd brought a wife back with him. But both of them being married didn't keep Travis and Grace from—"

She broke off for a moment and then said, "After Grace died, I thought that perhaps Greg— But no, he married that blond chit."

Chit seemed scarcely a word for the lovely but definitely middle-aged Caroline Woodhull. Twenty-five years ago, though, that somewhat derogatory term might have seemed appropriate, especially in the opinion of a bitterly disappointed woman.

She gave a short laugh and then said, "Well, maybe things even out. At least I'm still here. Travis Eaton is gone. Died of a heart attack while he was still in his thirties. Grace and her children went down with that boat about ten years later. And Gregory Woodhull, so I've heard, is in a wheelchair. But I'm not only still here, but going strong."

Again she gave that short laugh. "This is what comes of living alone and not seeing many people. When you do start talking you can't stop. Let that be a lesson to you, young woman."

I murmured something ambiguous. How much of what Doris Gowrey had said, I wondered, was true? How much was just the spite of a woman who had been cheated, not once, but twice, of her hopes of marrying the man she wanted? I didn't know, nor did I have any desire to sit in judgment on the tangled love relationships of others, especially relationships twenty-five years and more in the past. After all, it was not as if any of those involved had committed a crime—

A crime. A figure in a child's fantasy, stepping at night over a pleasure boat's rail—

Doris Gowrey interrupted my half-formed thought. "Then you definitely won't accept my offer?"

"No. But rest assured that I will take good care of your house."

The eyes behind the steel-rimmed glasses again had that odd brightness. "Then there is no point in our talking any longer, is there?"

"I suppose not," I said, reaching for the door handle. "Goodbye, Miss Gowrey."

I stepped out into the road. As the old car drove away I looked after it, feeling a mixture of emotions—resentment of Doris Gowrey's attitude toward me, and yet pity and distaste for a life that had been, apparently, spent largely in frustration and envy. I felt uneasy, too. But that was absurd. She couldn't put me out of this house.

I turned and went up the walk. By the time I'd finished my

breakfast in the sun-flooded dining room, I had ceased to think of Doris Gowrey.

Several days passed. Except for a few words exchanged with a checkout clerk at the supermarket or the proprietor of the laundromat in East Hampton, I spent those days in solitude and silence, keeping the house neat, sitting on the beach, which became a little more crowded each day, sometimes climbing the dune early in the evening to watch the stars come out. I did not see any of those three, but I sensed their friendly presence.

Then, one extremely hot afternoon as I entered the house, feeling relaxed and a little sunburned after two hours on the beach, the phone began to ring.

David's voice said, "Hello, Diana. Ready for a weekend guest?"

I echoed blankly, "Weekend?"

"Yes, you know. Those two days at the end of the week. They're called Saturday and Sunday, and people go away for them. I told you I'd come out there for a weekend as soon as I could, remember?"

"Then this is Friday?"

"Of course it's Friday! Have you relaxed so completely out there in lotus land that you don't even know what day it is?"

"I guess I just lost track."

An uncertain note came into his voice. "Is something wrong, Diana? Don't you want to see me?"

"Of course I do," I said after a moment. And I did. Just the sound of his voice made me realize how much I wanted to be with him, and to see the smile that deepened the sun wrinkles at the corners of his eyes, and feel the touch of his hands. But I was afraid, too, afraid that his coming here would mean some sort of loss—

"Fine," he said. "I'll be on the train that gets to Bridgehampton at seven-forty-five."

"I'll meet you."

When I'd hung up I stood there with my hand still on the phone. Something had changed in the last minute or so. Then I realized what it was. The house felt empty now.

Had they withdrawn behind some kind of barrier, a barrier

that just the prospect of David's presence had been enough to erect? Or were they no longer here?

A part of my mind said, "Of course they're not here, you fool. They never were." But that did not lessen my sense of loss.

Chapter 8

As I stood with my hand on the phone, it rang again. I lifted the instrument.

"Miss Garson?"

"Yes."

"This is the Hamptons Summer Services calling. You were on a list of new subscribers the phone company gave us, but of course you realize that your name will not be listed in the directory, not when you are only a summer subscriber. Now when your friends come out here from the city, wouldn't you like them to be able to get in touch with you?"

"What?"

"I know what you're about to say. You've already given your phone number to some friends, and others can get it from information. But how about people you may not even know are out here, people you'd like to see? Maybe they wouldn't know you are out here, either. But if they could look through a summer directory and see your name, they'd call you up, wouldn't they?"

"I'm afraid I don't see—"

"Now we're compiling a directory of summer people's phone numbers. It will be placed in railroad stations and supermarkets and motels and liquor stores, anyplace where friends of yours might open it and say, 'Why, Diana Garson is out here! Let's ask her to have dinner with us.' Now our charge for listing your name and number is only ten dollars, which is a small price to pay considering all the good times you might otherwise—"

"Thank you, but I'm not interested. No, really I'm not. Goodbye." I hung up.

Annoying as the phone call had been, it at least served to shake me out of my introspection. With a weekend guest arriving in a few hours, I had plenty to do. I went upstairs and made up the bed in that small room across the hall from mine. As I tucked sheets and two light blankets into place, I tried not to think about the difference I'd sensed in the atmosphere ever since David's phone call. I went down to the kitchen, made out a grocery list, and then drove to the liquor store and the supermarket in East Hampton.

On this afternoon, with people buying for the weekend, the supermarket checkout line was very long. Before joining it, I picked up a copy of the East Hampton *Star* from a rack near the counter. Standing behind my wire cart in the slow-moving line, I opened the paper and began to read.

On an inside page I saw the headline: "Springs Man Arrested for Drunk Driving." My eye was about to pass over the story when a vaguely familiar name, Larry Philbeam, caught my attention. Hadn't I somewhere, recently— Of course. He was mentioned in that old *Star* clipping about the dinner honoring Derek Woodhull's service in Korea. Also, according to the captions written by Grace Woodhull, Larry Philbeam was in several of the snapshots taken in Korea. I read:

Larry Philbeam, 49, of Widow Winthrop's Path, Springs, was arrested last Tuesday after the unlicensed car he was driving collided with a telephone pole on Montauk Highway. Charged with drunken driving and operating an unlicensed vehicle, Philbeam was unable to post bail and is now being held pending his court appearance.

Philbeam has a record of a number of arrests for drunken driving and for disorderly conduct. Last March he was arrested for assault after his common-law wife, Birdie, 36, complained that he had beaten her. When she withdrew the charges, Philbeam was released.

I knew vaguely that Springs, a part of East Hampton township, was a still-rural community where a number of artists and actors and writers lived, some of them world famous. But I also had heard that on its back roads, in unpainted shacks, lived the local equivalents of Ozark hillbillies, inbred ne'er-do-wells who, since many of them were descendants of pre-Revolutionary Long Islanders, often bore names that also belonged to highly respected people in the community. Philbeam, evidently, was such a name. There was a Philbeam Road out here, and a Philbeam Pond, and a Philbeam Construction Company, and a Philbeam Horse Farm.

If this man was the Lieutenant Larry Philbeam of those old snapshots—and the age given in the newspaper would indicate that he probably was—what had happened to him? How was it that he had ended up on a Springs back road with a common-law wife, who had charged him with assault? The woman ahead of me had reached the checker now. I began to lift my groceries from the wire basket to the counter.

I was about to turn off Montauk Highway onto the road that led through Quogsett when I realized that I had bought nothing —neither cheese and crackers nor anything else—to accompany the vodka and tonic I planned to serve. I glanced at my watch. Almost six. No time to return to East Hampton. I would have to stop at the store in Quogsett, even though it might mean running into Beth Warren. A few minutes later I saw that her red Datsun stood in front of her office. Well, perhaps I still could do my shopping and drive off without her seeing me.

I had just started up the general store steps when its door opened and Beth came out, slipping a pack of cigarettes into her brown straw shoulder bag. We both halted. She said, "Why, hello, Diana." Then, lowering her voice: "You're not still shopping for groceries here, are you? The supermarkets in East Hampton and Southampton are much cheaper."

"I know. But when I was in East Hampton I forgot to buy anything to serve as canapés."

"So! Guests for cocktails, or maybe dinner?"

"David Corway is coming for the weekend."

I saw a wry expression in her eyes. Was she remembering

long-past weekends that David Corway had spent out here? "Give him my love."

I nodded. Then, unable to resist voicing my resentment, I said, "Doris Gowrey came to see me a few days ago."

"I know. She dropped by my office after she'd seen you. I'm sorry about the whole thing. But when she phoned me the night before I had to tell her who'd rented her house, didn't I? I mean, when she asked how old you were, and whether you were single or married, I had to tell her the truth."

"I suppose so." But you needn't have told her, I added mentally, what I'd said about the atmosphere of that house. Since you've been her agent for a number of years, you must know what she's like. You must have realized she would jump to the conclusion that I'd take the bread out of her mouth by telling everyone her house was haunted.

I started past her, and then turned back. "By the way, do you happen to know a Larry Philbeam?"

"There are lots of Philbeams out here."

"This one is in the *Star* this week. He was arrested for drunk driving."

"Oh, that Philbeam. He's always in the police news."

"Did you know him a long time ago, that first summer you were out here?"

"Why do you ask?"

Hostility in her face now. I wasn't surprised. She had made it clear that she didn't like reminders of the days when she was Elizabeth Bratianu. But then, she had not been considerate of me in the Doris Gowrey matter. And, as always, there was this need, indefinable but urgent, to learn all I could about those three who had vanished a quarter of a century ago.

I said, "That album. Larry Philbeam was in some of those snapshots taken in Korea."

Her voice was cool. "I don't remember actually meeting him in those days, but I do remember hearing his name. Once I overheard Mrs. Woodhull talking about him to the Warrens."

"What was she saying?"

"How can you expect me to remember? I wasn't even eleven years old then! But it was something about the war in Korea.

Something that had happened over there, which made Mrs. Woodhull's son stop being friends with Larry Philbeam."

"What had happened?"

"I don't know. In fact, I remember now. That was the whole point. Mrs. Woodhull's son wouldn't talk about it, and that annoyed her." She added, "So you're still hung up on those pictures of people you never even knew."

Mockery had come into her voice. Perhaps she hoped it would sound like friendly mockery, but it did not. Hung up, I thought. I was far more than that. If she or anyone else knew what I had experienced—or thought I had experienced—in that ordinary-looking house beside the dune, they would say I was mad. And perhaps, I thought, suddenly miserable, I was.

"Oh," I said, "I just couldn't help being curious about Larry Philbeam. Well, so long," I added, moving past her, "I'd better get my shopping done."

As I approached the Bridgehampton station a few minutes past seven-thirty that evening, I became aware of more evidence than the humid heat that the summer season was here. The station platform, almost empty when I had driven past it at this hour about a week before, was now crowded with people. Most of them were wives and children waiting to greet Daddy when he arrived after his week of toil in the city. But there were others, too, ranging from prosperous-looking retirees, perhaps there to meet arriving children or grandchildren, to people of college age, many of them in tennis clothes.

The train pulled in, with some of its windows bearing star-shaped cracks inflicted by rock-throwing small boys, and its vestibules crowded with city-pale people eager to descend. When the train finally stopped I was standing at a point about midway of its length. Thus I saw David, who got out of the next to last coach, before he saw me. My heart lifted. I had forgotten how attractive he was, sturdy and yet with an athlete's easy grace, his square-chinned face now, as always, tanned, his blue eyes searching the platform for me. And yet for a long time now—ten days? more?—I'd scarcely given him a thought.

He had seen me. His face lit up with a gladness that left me shaken. I had known he was fond of me. After all, I was that nice girl downstairs, always a pleasant partner for dinner or a movie or a game of chess. But had he, while I was out here, discovered that he was fonder of me than he had realized?

We moved toward each other. When we were about twenty feet apart I saw his expression change. He still smiled, but anxiety had come into his eyes. He set down his brown leather suitcase, tilted my chin, and kissed me.

"Hello, lotus eater." He still smiled, but a frown had creased his forehead. "Looks to me as if you haven't been eating much else. You've lost weight, you know."

"Have I? Well, I haven't had much appetite lately." I realized now that, except for my first few days in that house, I hadn't bothered to prepare full meals for myself.

When we reached the car he asked if I wanted him to drive, and I said yes. We drove down Bridgehampton's main street and then turned to our right along a street of nineteenth-century houses set far back on well-kept lawns. As he talked of the uncomfortable train ride—the air-conditioning had broken down in his coach—he kept glancing at me from the corner of his eye. Finally he said, "There's something wrong, isn't there?"

"I guess so." Suddenly I realized just how much I wanted to tell him about it.

"What is it?"

"Maybe I could talk better if we pulled over to the side of the road."

We parked beside a giant elm, midway between two houses. I said, "I think it started the night I moved in. I heard voices and the sound of a girl's laugh. But I decided it was just people who'd stayed late on the beach and then walked past the house on the way to their car."

Sometimes haltingly, sometimes speaking with a rush, I told him of those three who, even though they might be just shadows produced by my imagination, seemed so very real to me. I told him of how, even when I did not see them or hear them, a sense of their presence brought me a calm, almost dreamlike content. I didn't look at David's face as I talked, but now and then I glanced at his hand, gripping the wheel. His whitened knuckles told me how appalled he was.

At last I forced myself to look at his face. "You think I'm crazy, don't you?"

His voice was grim. "I certainly don't think those people of yours are real. Whether or not that makes you crazy, I don't know. I'm no expert. But one thing I'm sure of. You're going to stay out of that house for at least a few hours. We'll go to a restaurant for dinner."

"But I've bought everything! Lamb chops, salad, vegetables, wine, vodka, everything."

"It'll keep."

"And look how I'm dressed." Because of the heat, I wore yellow cotton shorts and a matching shirt.

"This is the Hamptons, remember. There are plenty of places between here and Montauk, not fancy but with good food. They won't care what you wear."

We drove several miles east to a bustling, well-lighted seafood place. Many of the tables were occupied by family groups. Throughout the meal David did most of the talking, telling me about his architectural firm's progress on its latest rush job, and about a campaign the tenants' committee in our apartment house was waging to get new street lights on our block. Neither of us mentioned what I had told him, but I'm sure that he was thinking of little else, just as I was.

When he had called for the check he said, "Now we'll go to a disco."

"A disco! Why, first I'd have to go back to the house and—"

"No. There's a place in Westhampton that I'm sure will let us in."

"Westhampton! Why, that's about twenty miles from—"

"What do we care?"

I suppose he meant to speak lightly, but it came out grim. Plainly he was determined to surround me for a few hours with as much light and noise as possible. Well, perhaps that wasn't surprising. Perhaps he was reverting to the ancient faith in glare and loud sounds to dispel supernatural forces. For instance, there were the Chinese with their fireworks and cymbals.

And if I wasn't mistaken, I reflected unhappily, in some cultures people regarded shouting, drumbeating, and a general up-roar as ways of curing the mad.

We drove twenty miles through hot darkness. Sometimes, when there was a break in the stream of headlights coming to-ward us on the opposite side of the highway, I saw in the fields on either side the drifting, green-white glow of fireflies.

The disco was housed in what once had been a potato barn. We parked the VW and then joined the line of people seeking admission. David had been right. In this motley crowd, my infor-mal attire would be no problem. True, some of those in the line were dressed like patrons of the most posh Manhattan discos, the girls in slithery silks and flimsy sandals, the men in tight pants and open-to-the-navel satin shirts. Other patrons of both sexes, though, were dressed in shorts or jeans or chinos.

We went inside. Throbbing music and light enfolded us. From the table assigned to us on the gallery that ran around two sides of the room, the dance floor was a seething mass of gyrating bodies and upflung arms. We descended the stairs several times to dance. I did not enjoy it. In fact, after days of silence and soli-tude, the close-packed crowd and the ear-splitting music and the flashing strobes seemed almost unbearable. Not even the several drinks I consumed served to numb me to the uproar. My head began to ache. Around midnight I asked David to take me home.

We said little as the VW, with David at the wheel, carried us back over the twenty miles. Now that cars were fewer, the drift-ing glow of fireflies over the potato fields shone brighter. The temperature had dropped only a little. The night was still so hot that we might as well have been driving along Manhattan's Third Avenue, rather than through farmland, with the sea never more than a mile or so away.

When we reached the house he did not turn in toward the ga-rage but stopped out in the road. "Let's go swimming. It will help your headache."

"All right," I said, opening the car door. "I'll change into—"

"No!" His hand fastened around my wrist. "No need to go into the house yet. You've got something on under your shirt and shorts, haven't you? And I'll take my terry-cloth robe out of my suitcase. We can both use that as a towel."

We walked past the dune onto the beach. There had been a waning half moon earlier, but it had set. Now the darkness was relieved only by the stars, dim through the heat haze, and the pale glimmer of low, foaming waves moving toward shore. David stripped to shorts, and I to panties and bra. The water seemed cold only for a few seconds. After that it was a delight, sliding with a champagnelike tingle through my hair and along my face and body.

After a while David asked, swimming beside me in the trough between two waves, "Had enough?"

We moved up onto the beach. A few yards beyond the water's edge we stopped and toweled ourselves with the terry-cloth robe. Then David spread the robe on the sand and we sat down.

After a moment he said, "You can't go on staying in that house, you know."

Just as when Beth Warren and Doris Gowrey had tried to get me out of that house, my resistance rose. In fact, it was even stronger now than before. "I don't want to leave! I've been happy here."

As I said the words, I realized how true they were. I had been happier here, happier than during the years of my growing up in Aunt Gertrude's silent house, happier than during all but the first months of my marriage, happier than I'd been the past winter, falling deeper and deeper in love with a man who led his girls past my door on the way to his own apartment.

"Happy!" His voice was scathing. "So were the lotus eaters, so happy that they forgot everything and everyone who was part of their past lives. I was right to call you a lotus eater. Diana, you're in love with those people you've imagined, particularly that—what was his name?—Derek Woodhull. You're in love with a guy whose picture you saw in an old album, a guy who's been dead for twenty-five years!"

One of his arms went around my shoulders. His other hand, thumb and forefinger pressing into my cheeks, held my face. His kiss was far from gentle. Then he was bearing me backward onto the robe and the soft sand beneath it. I felt his fingers briefly, expertly, unfastening the hooks of my bra.

I wanted him, wanted him desperately. But not like this. Not when I was aware that more than physical desire drove him. Not when I knew that he wanted to possess, not just my body, but what he thought of as my obsessed mind. And so I fought him, twisting my face away from his lips, pressing one hand against his hard shoulder, trying with the other to arrest the movements of his hand over my body.

After several moments of that silent struggle, I heard him mutter something. He rolled away from me and sat up. Heart pounding, I, too, sat up. For a while we sat side by side, saying nothing. Then David said, in a harsh voice, "Sorry."

Because I still felt the ache of thwarted desire, it cost me an effort to speak. "It's all right."

"It wasn't just that I wanted you," he went on, "although of course I've wanted you since I first saw you. But tonight I wanted— Well, call it kind of an attempt at exorcism. I want you to be rid of that house, rid of those—those—"

"I can't leave the house."

"For God's sake, Diana, why not?"

I struggled to explain. "It's this feeling I have. Unless I'm just crazy, there's a *reason* for what's happened to me here. I can't leave until I know what the reason is. I—I guess once I could have left. But I feel that if I tried to now I'd just—go to pieces entirely. It's as if I've been swimming a river, and I'm now past the halfway point. Maybe I can make the far shore. But if I try to turn back I'll surely drown."

After a moment he said heavily, "What I'd like to do is haul you back to New York by force. But of course I can't do that."

We dressed in silence. Up on the narrow road he asked, "Shall I run the car into the garage?"

"There's no need to."

He took his suitcase from the car's trunk and we both went up the walk. When I had unlocked the door and we had gone inside I flipped on the hall light. He looked down at me. "Well?" he said, meaning, Do you feel them, are they here?

I shook my head. If they were here, they had withdrawn behind that barrier.

"Of course," he said, meaning, Of course they're not here; they never were.

I led him up the stairs. When we reached the small bedroom opposite mine, he opened the door, felt inside for the switch, and turned on the light. "I see the bed's made up. Is this where I sleep?"

I nodded. "Good-night, David."

"Good-night." He went inside and closed the door.

Chapter 9

I awoke to the sound of a brisk wind rattling the old window frames and to the smell of frying bacon. After a confused moment I realized that David must be cooking his breakfast. I reached for the watch I had placed on the stand beside my bed and saw that it was past ten. Well, that wasn't surprising. I'd lain awake for a long time the night before, feeling confused and wretched, acutely aware of David's presence in the room across the hall, and almost equally aware of that certain emptiness in the atmosphere.

The wind had swept yesterday's sultriness away. Despite this morning's bright sunlight, the air was almost cool. I dressed in jeans and a T-shirt and went down to the kitchen. With a plate of bacon and scrambled eggs in his hand, David turned away from the stove.

"Good morning. I didn't want to disturb you, so I made my own breakfast. I hope you don't mind." His expression, like his words, was carefully polite.

"Of course not."

"Can I fix you something?"

"No, thanks." I looked at the percolator bubbling on the stove. "I'll just pour myself a cup of coffee."

For a few moments we sat in silence, facing each other across the kitchen table. Then he said, "I phoned Jack Kluger about an hour ago." Kluger was another of the partners in David's architectural firm. "He said that something had come up, and that I'd better get back to town, even if it is a Saturday."

A lie. But after I had rebuffed both his lovemaking and his pleas that I leave this house, I could scarcely tell him that he lied. I said, "I'll drive you to the station."

"No need. Beth Warren called about half an hour ago. She said you told her yesterday that I'd be here. Maybe you heard the phone ring."

"No, I didn't."

"Anyway, she phoned. She said she'd just wanted to say hello. I told her that I'd been called back to New York, and she offered to drive me to the train. She's picking me up at eleven."

And on the way to the station, no doubt, he would tell her all that I'd told him last night, and urge her to find some way of getting me out of this house. Well, let her try. I'd paid my forty-five-hundred dollars.

"Very well," I said.

We were both waiting in the living room when Beth drove up in the red Datsun. I accompanied him down the walk. Beth said, "Good morning, Diana, David."

Her eyes had a pleased shine. Although engaged to Winstead Chalmers, and desperately eager to hold onto him, she still was interested enough in David to feel gratified that my weekend with him had been cut short.

He opened the Datsun's rear door and placed his suitcase inside. "Thank you, Diana," he said, turning to me. "Sorry things turned out like this."

By "this," I knew, he meant far more than his sudden departure. He kissed me briefly, went around to the other side of the car, and got in beside Beth. The little car backed, made a U-turn, and drove away over the rutted road. For a moment or two I stood looking after it. Then, aware that Beth might be watching me in the rearview mirror, I turned and went into the house.

For perhaps fifteen minutes I sat in the silent living room. The house still felt empty. It was if the barrier erected by David's hostile, skeptical presence was so strong that it remained in place even after he had gone.

I felt a sudden need to get away, miles away. I climbed the stairs, picked up my shoulder bag and a sweater, and went out to the VW.

I drove clear to Montauk, over a long stretch where farmlands gave way to heather-clad soil, which people often compared to that of Scotland, then over high, pine-covered land from which I could see the Atlantic on my right and Long Island Sound on my left, both flecked with whitecaps on this windy day. When I reached Montauk I stopped at a quick-lunch place for a cheese sandwich and coffee, and then drove out to the high point from which the lighthouse rose. Standing there, looking out over water, which, I knew, stretched unbroken to the European shore, I tried to force myself to think clearly, to weigh my need for David—sane, tough-minded David, who perhaps was fonder of me than either of us had realized—against the strange bond that held me to that house and to those shadowy three who, perhaps, were only creatures of my own mind. But my thought processes were sluggish, confused, almost as if I had eaten of that fabled lotus David had mentioned.

At last I drove back slowly, through waning afternoon light. I stopped off at a little fishing marina and looked at the boats tied up at the wharf and wandered through a little art gallery filled with indifferent paintings of Long Island scenes. A few miles east of Bridgehampton I stopped again and had a hamburger at a roadside diner. When I came out I found that it was twilight now, and that the wind, which had died down in midafternoon, had picked up again. By the time I reached the road paralleling the dunes, wind was bending the fields of potato plants, their white blossoms ghostly in the gloom, and twisting trees in the yards of the few houses I passed. I turned onto the narrow dirt road leading to the beach.

When I'd put the car in the garage I entered the house by the back door and walked along the hall through the near darkness. With no idea that I was going to do so, I halted abruptly at the foot of the stairs. After two or three seconds I turned and walked into the living room.

They were there. Grace Woodhull turned from the front window to smile at me. Derek and Sheila, standing beside the tall phonograph, also smiled.

Grace Woodhull said, "Hello, Diana."

I said, "Why?"

She seemed to know immediately what I meant. "Why are we here? Why do you see us? Is that what you're asking?"

Feeling a dreamlike numbness, I nodded.

"We're here because we didn't want to die," Mrs. Woodhull said, "and because it wasn't an accident that caused us to die."

"No," Derek said, "it was no accident."

I looked at him from the corner of my eye and saw that neither he nor Sheila was smiling now. Mrs. Woodhull said, "Shouldn't murder be revealed?" She, too, was no longer smiling.

After a moment she asked, "You're not afraid of us, are you, Diana?"

"No," I said, but that wasn't true. I knew what they wanted of me now, and for a moment I was terribly afraid. Then the numb, dreamlike feeling came back.

Mrs. Woodhull said, "You're tired, aren't you? Perhaps you'd better go to bed."

"Yes," I said, and turned away.

In the big bedroom upstairs I undressed. I think that, despite the wind whining around the corner of the house, I fell asleep almost as soon as I got into bed.

A flickering through my closed eyelids awakened me. My eyes flew open. Reddish light danced on the opposite wall of the darkened bedroom.

Fire. Somewhere outside. Somewhere close.

I swung out of bed, snatched up my dark flannel robe from a chairback. Struggling into the robe, I ran to the window. The source of that rosy, dancing light seemed to come from the rear of the house, beyond my line of vision.

Aware of racing heartbeats, aware that wind still rattled the old window frames, I turned and moved swiftly out of the room and down the length of the hall. The rear door was closed but unlocked. I moved out onto the narrow second-floor balcony.

It was that tall old incinerator, down there between the garage and the dry cement basin of the wading pool. Crammed with trash I had intended to take to the dump, the incinerator somehow had caught fire. Flames rose in a spiral that bent this way and that in the wind. Sparks and bits of flaming paper flew through the air.

As I stood with my hands gripping the low rail, I heard a siren's wail, and saw headlights speeding along the road that paralleled the line of dunes. So someone, probably an occupant of one of the few houses along that road, had called the fire department. I felt mingled relief and chagrin. After all, a few buckets of water could have doused a blazing incinerator. Or I could have just let it burn itself out.

The fire engine had turned onto the narrow road that led to this house. Just how, I wondered, had the incinerator caught fire? Certainly I hadn't lit it.

Then my heart leaped with fear. Wind-driven sparks and bits of flaming trash streamed toward the house now. A large, fiery fragment flew over my head. Almost certainly that had landed on the roof. How much more flaming material had come to rest on those dry old shingles?

I turned back into the house and slammed the door shut lest sparks and bits of flaming matter land in the upstairs hall. Then, pausing only to flip a light switch, I hurried down the stairs, back along the ground-floor hall, through the dark kitchen. I had just emerged onto the weedy, hard-packed sand when the fire truck turned in beside the house. Right behind it was the tank truck with its long, cylindrical body.

I stood aside while helmeted men tumbled down off the halted trucks. "Get the roof first, Joe," I heard one of them say. I looked up and saw, not flames, thank heaven, but the glow of several smouldering patches on the steeply pitched roof.

The hurrying men attached a big canvas hose to the tank truck. A stream of water arched up onto the roof. Dimly aware that the sky had taken on a dawn gray, I watched with relief as one glowing spot after another disappeared.

A police car had turned in behind the fire trucks. Its uniformed driver got out and spoke to one of the firemen who stood leaning, arms crossed, against the lead truck. The men with the hose, now that the roof was all right, had turned their attention to the incinerator. Soon there were no more flames, just a soggy black mess inside the incinerator and on the ground around it. Provokingly, the wind had died to a fitful breeze, now that the fire was out.

Two firemen came out the back door. With my anxious gaze fastened on the roof, I hadn't been aware that they had gone inside the house. "It's okay," one of them said to the man leaning against the truck. Then, to me, "We wanted to make sure that there were no smouldering spots on the underside of the roof. There aren't. The house smells a little smoky now, but otherwise everything is okay."

I thanked the firemen. The police car backed out, and then the two fire trucks, their headlights pale in the dawn light. I expected the police car to follow the firemen up the road, but it did not. Its driver, a paunchy man of late middle age, walked toward me. He had what looked like a leather-covered notebook in his hand.

"You the tenant?"

"Yes."

"I'm Jim McPheeters, Southampton Town Police." He flipped open the notebook and I saw it contained a pad of printed forms. "Name?"

"Why? What is this?"

"Fraid I'll have to give you a summons. Burning trash is against the law. You're supposed to take it to the dump."

"I know that. And I didn't burn it. I don't know how it caught fire."

"Kids, maybe. These days some of them are out helling around even at three and four in the morning. But I'll have to give you a summons anyway."

"I don't see why. If I didn't—"

"Look, lady, it's not a hanging offense. Even if the judge thinks you're guilty he won't fine you more than a few dollars."

"I don't see how he could think that I'd get up at three in the morning to burn trash!"

"Well, some folks too lazy to cart trash to the dump do try to get away with burning it at night. That is, if they live in an isolated place, they do. Probably, though, the judge will believe you. But I have to give you a summons. Now what's the name?"

I told him. He filled out the summons and, with an apology, handed it to me. I watched him drive away and then opened the back door.

The firemen had been right. The house smelled smoky. Leaving the back door open, I hurried upstairs and began raising windows. In my bedroom I paused long enough to dress. The high winds of yesterday and last night evidently had been a weather front, bringing cool air behind it. This morning I added to my jeans not a T-shirt but a blue turtleneck sweater. Then I went down the stairs and opened windows on the ground floor. As I moved about I was aware that the house again had that empty feeling, as if the invasion of fire-helmeted men had caused those shadowy three to withdraw. Finally, leaving the front door open, I went out onto the porch and sat down on the top step. The wind had died entirely. Overhead pink and gold clouds hung almost motionless in the tender morning sky.

For perhaps half an hour, there in the cool morning, I enjoyed a kind of respite. Deep in my mind the troubled thoughts swirled. The fiasco of my weekend with David, a weekend that otherwise might have been the start of something important for both of us. That encounter that I had had—or thought I had had?—in the half-darkened living room the night before. The fire, which had seemed to start all by itself. But for a while the surface of my mind was calm, calm as the new morning, with early sunlight now flooding the potato fields across the road.

The sound of an approaching car made me turn my head. As it drew close I saw that it was Doris Gowrey's well-kept old sedan. It stopped in front of the house. This time she did not sound the horn. She got out and moved up the walk, erect and strong looking, despite her deeply lined face. She was wearing the same green and white dress she'd had on the first time I saw her. More curious than apprehensive, I stood up and walked down the steps to meet her.

She said, "Miss Garson, I'd thank you kindly to leave my house as soon as you can pack."

"No doubt you would thank me for leaving." Somehow my calm persisted. "But I do not intend to leave. We went over that the other day. I refused your offer."

"I'm not renewing the offer. Now you won't get the whole forty-five-hundred back. I'll deduct for the time you've been here. You're lucky I've got insurance. Otherwise I'd charge you for repairing the roof."

I said, amazed, "You've heard about the incinerator this soon?"

"I get up very early, Miss Garson, and I tune in WLNG as soon as it comes on the air. They had the news about the fire and about the summons Jim McPheeters gave you."

I wasn't surprised that my incinerator fire had been reported on the air. Sometimes I'd tuned my transistor to the station in nearby Sag Harbor, and I'd discovered that when news was meager almost anything on the police blotters of the various villages was considered worthy of air time—a fender-bending accident in a Southampton parking lot, a juvenile charged with breaking a window in Bridgehampton, or a Sag Harbor man accused of letting his Labrador retriever chase ducks on Otter Pond.

I said, "You can't evict me for something that wasn't my fault."

"Miss Garson, did you read the rental contract you signed? There's a clause that says tenants can be evicted not only for damaging the property, but for violating any local ordinance while on the property."

I felt rising alarm and indignation. "But I didn't light that incinerator!"

"I think the judge will say you did."

Who was the judge before whom I'd appear? Was he, like herself, a native? Probably. He might even be a relative of hers.

"Better pack, Miss Garson. I want you out of here by this afternoon. I'll drop by Beth Warren's office, so that she'll have your refund check ready for you."

"Miss Gowrey!" I was trembling with anger now, anger and panic. I could not leave, not yet. As I had told David, I felt that if I were wrenched away from this house now, I would shatter completely.

"If you try to force me out, I'll take it to court," I said. "And I will talk about this hours to reporters or to anyone else who will listen. Haunted houses make good newspaper copy," I went on recklessly. "Look at that one in Amityville."

Would I, if she had pressed me too hard, have carried out that threat? I don't know. Probably not. But the point was that she believed I might do it.

Her face was pale now. "I think I'll sit down." She walked past me to the porch and, as I turned to face her, sank down on the middle step. She asked heavily, "Then you really have seen things in this house?"

"Not things. People."

She didn't ask what people, which made me think that she already knew, or at least guessed. Instead she said, half to herself, "No one else, not in all the years this house has been rented out each summer—"

"I know. You told me that the last time you were here."

The gray eyes behind the steel-rimmed glasses considered me. "Then it's you. Either you're crazy or—"

She broke off. I didn't speak. After a moment she said, still pale, but more composed now, "I'll make a bargain with you. You can stay if you'll allow Mrs. Conski to stay here with you."

"Mrs. who?"

"Conski. She was my cleaning woman until she hurt her back in a fall a few months ago. She's about to lose the room she occupied all last winter. It's been rented to a couple of summer people at a much higher rate."

I remained silent, nonplussed. Did she think that with another person in the house I might not, in her phrase, "see things"? If so, she might be right about that. Even the prospect of David's presence had brought me a sense that those others had withdrawn. I had told him so. Had he told that to Beth Warren as she drove him to the station the morning before, and had she passed the information on to Doris Gowrey?

"Mrs. Conski won't be any expense to you," Doris Gowrey went on. "She has enough to pay for her food. And she won't bother you. She seldom says anything at all unless you ask her a question.

"You'd better say yes, Miss Garson," she added. "Otherwise I'll evict you, no matter what stories you threaten to circulate."

Was *she* bluffing now? I looked at the hard glitter of the eyes behind the steel-rimmed glasses and knew that I didn't want to take the chance.

Nevertheless, I temporized for a moment. "Just why do you want this woman to move in here with me?"

"Quite frankly, Miss Garson, I want someone to keep an eye on you. I don't think that's surprising, not after this fire. Why, my house could have burned to the ground." She raised her hand, palm outward, like a traffic cop. "Oh, I know! You told me the fire wasn't your fault. Just the same, I want Mrs. Conski to move in here." She paused. "Well, Miss Garson?"

I said, "All right."

"Good." Grunting slightly, she rose from the step. "She'll be here right away."

When she had driven off, with no farewell but a curt nod, I went around the corner of the house and looked at the mess the firemen had left: pieces of blackened, soggy paper scattered among the weeds and over the cracked basin of the old wading pool. A blackened mass about three feet high in the incinerator itself.

There was a rusty old garbage can in the garage and an equally rusty shovel and rake. I brought them out and set to work, first forcing the incinerator, still faintly warm, onto its side, and shoveling the mess into the garbage can. Cleaning up the yard proved more difficult. The blackened fragments of paper broke when I tried to rake them, and I finally had to grub up the pieces with my hands. I had almost finished the job when an ancient gray sedan rattled down the road and turned in beside the house. A woman was at the wheel.

Doris Gowrey hadn't exaggerated when she said that Mrs. Conski would be here "right away."

The driver opened the car door, which had been dented badly at some time in the past, and got out, her thick body bent slightly from the waist. She reached back onto the seat, brought out an old leather suitcase bound with a length of cord and set it on the ground. Then she turned to me.

Coarse dark hair. A face out of van Gogh's "The Potato Eaters." Stolid, earthy, stubbornly enduring.

"Missis?"

I said uncertainly, "Yes?" Later I realized that probably she addressed all her employers in that way. I wasn't her employer, but that was all she ever called me.

"I'm Mary Conski."

"How do you do? I'm Diana Garson. Shall we go in?"

Carrying her suitcase, she followed me in through the back door and the kitchen and up the stairs. There I hesitated. Somehow I didn't want to put her in the room David had occupied, even though it had been for only one night.

I opened the door of the second small bedroom. It was a nice room. Floral wallpaper with a yellow background, only a little faded. A large oval rag rug, its colors muted by many washings, on the wide-boarded floor. A spool bed of pine, its mattress bare, and a matching chest of drawers and dressing table. "Will this do? We'll make up the bed, of course."

She nodded, face expressionless, and set down her suitcase.

Unnerved by her silence, I began to chatter. "We'll have to share the bath, since there's only one. As for meals, well, we can sit down and list what we both like, and then figure out how to arrange—"

"No need to talk about it, missis. I buy my own food and cook my own meals. You do the same with yours."

Chapter 10

Days passed. Mrs. Conski rose at daybreak, breakfasted at six, ate lunch at eleven, and finished her supper by five. She took all her meals in the kitchen, and left the room spotless. Most of the rest of the time she stayed in her bedroom. To my knowledge, she never entered the living room or dining room, although sometimes she did sit on the porch in the wicker rocker and look out over the potato fields across the road. Since she seldom spoke unless I spoke to her, and even then answered as briefly as possible, the squeaking of that rocker was about the loudest noise she made. It was rather like living with Aunt Gertrude, except that I had always known that Aunt Gertrude loved me, and it was hard to imagine someone as wooden as Mrs. Conski ever loving—or hating—anyone.

Three days after the incinerator fire a carpenter came to repair the roof, hammered for a couple of hours, and departed. The next day, the date specified on my summons, I went to Southampton and appeared before a magistrate there. A gaunt, lantern-jawed man, he might well have been a relative of Doris Gowrey's. I explained that I had no idea how the incinerator had caught fire. He nodded. "Kids," he said, and added, "Case dismissed."

That same day, early in the evening, David phoned. "Are you all right, Diana?"

"Yes, David."

There was a silence. Then I said, "I know what you called up to ask. You want to know about the—the Woodhulls. You want to know if I see them now. The answer is no."

When he didn't speak, I added, "There is a woman living with me now, a Mrs. Conski."

"There is? How did that happen?"

A certain falsity in his tone. I felt quite sure that he had been in touch with Beth Warren, and that she had told him about the fire and about Mary Conski's presence in this house. Nevertheless, I answered his question.

Finally he said, "And, since she moved in, there hasn't been—"

"No." That wasn't quite accurate. I still had a sense of them behind the barrier erected by Mary Conski's stolid presence. I had a sense, too, of their demand upon me, their urgent demand—

"Diana, let me come out there next weekend."

"No, David."

I wanted him and needed him more than I ever had. But the fiasco of those less than eighteen hours he had spent out here with me had convinced me of one thing. Whatever the Woodhulls were, whether entities in their own right or merely creatures of my own mind, I had no right to David's love until I was free of them. And I could not be free, I felt, until I had accomplished what they desired.

After several seconds, he said quietly, "All right, Diana. I'll call again soon."

Because I could not bear the altered atmosphere of the house, I took to spending most of the daylight hours outdoors. I swam and sunned myself. Twice more I clammed, the first time offering part of my catch to Mary Conski, who said, "They don't set right with me, missis." I visited art galleries for miles around.

But that only took care of the days. At night the barrier seemed thinner. I would lie awake, aware of their urgency like some tormenting need of my own. And yet how could I answer that need, when communication between us had been blocked, leaving me still with almost no knowledge of what had happened that night twenty-five years ago on a small boat off the Massachusetts coast?

When one night the realization came to me. People who believed in psychic manifestations also believed that there were ways to get through the barriers.

That woman at the East Hampton library—she had been kind, and as helpful as she could be. Perhaps she would be a good person for me to turn to now.

I entered the library the next morning a few minutes after it opened. To my relief, I saw that the same woman sat behind the desk. She was stamping several books for a stout woman in a green pantsuit and a wide straw hat of lighter green. I waited until the woman in the pantsuit had turned from the desk, her arms filled with books, and walked away. Then I said to the librarian, "Do you remember me? I was in here not long ago asking about books on the occult."

"Of course I remember. What can I do for you now?"

I said, feeling my throat tighten up with the lie, "I'm planning this book on psychic phenomena, and since you were so helpful the other day—well, I wondered if you knew whether or not there is a medium here in the Hamptons, or if you could tell me how I could find out."

"A medium?" The librarian's face wore an odd mixture of curiosity and embarrassed amusement. I had the feeling that she hadn't believed my lie. "I don't think you'd find anyone like that in the Hamptons."

I mumbled some sort of thanks and turned away. It was then I saw that the woman in green had not left the building. She was reading the notices on a bulletin board that stood near the door. I hurried past her.

I had reached the sidewalk when I heard someone call, "Miss!"

I turned and watched the woman in green come the rest of the way down the steps. She said, "I couldn't help overhearing what you asked the librarian."

Aware of humiliated color in my cheeks, I said, "Yes?"

"I know of someone. A black woman in Riverhead. She isn't really black. Light brown, I'd say. But these days you're supposed to say black. Anyway, she's awfully good. When my sister's husband died suddenly, no one in the family knew where the key to his safety deposit box was. Finally my sister went to this medium, and she told her where to find it. It had fallen off his key chain into a crack in the front walk."

"What's her name?"

"The medium? Mrs. Fell, Irene Fell. She lives on Gravin Street in Riverhead. I don't know the exact number, but you could look it up in the Suffolk County phone book."

"Thank you. Perhaps I'll go to see her."

I left my car where it was and walked a hundred yards or so north on Main Street to a drugstore. According to the phone book in the booth, Irene Fell lived at One-twenty-seven Gravin Street.

Riverhead is about twenty-five miles from East Hampton. Despite the summertime traffic—sightseeing vacationers dawdling along at thirty miles an hour, clanking combines and other farm machinery, trucks of all kinds—I managed to get there in forty minutes. According to the map given me a couple of weeks before by a filling station operator, Gravin Street was directly off Main Street. I had no trouble finding Gravin Street, or One-twenty-seven, either. It was a turn-of-the-century brown bungalow, its roof and side shingles in good repair, its lawn neatly mowed. Beds of marigolds, well-weeded and healthy looking, edged the walk that led up to the deep porch.

My ring was answered after a few seconds by a tall, good-looking woman of forty-odd. Her skin was a coppery brown, her features strong but regular, her expression dignified, perhaps even a bit disdainful. She wore a paisley-patterned housecoat. A scarf of the same pattern was wound around her head.

"Mrs. Fell?"

She nodded.

"My name is Diana Garson. You were recommended to me by—" Oh, why hadn't I asked the name of the woman in the green pantsuit? "By a woman who lives in East Hampton."

Apparently incurious as to the woman's identity, she asked, "What is it you want?"

Taken aback by her directness, I did not reply. She said, "A reading?"

"I'm not sure. I mean, I—I don't want my fortune told, or anything like that."

"Then you want to get in touch with someone who's passed on?"

How vulgar it sounded, put like that, how evocative of those depressed-looking women in New York, toiling up narrow stairs to gypsy tearooms. Nevertheless, I nodded.

"Come in."

The front door opened directly into the living room. Because of the depth of the porch, the room was shadowed, but there was enough light for me to see that it was as neat as the lawn and flower beds. The brown wall-to-wall carpeting looked old, the floral-patterned sofa and matching armchair fairly new. On one wall a brightly colored print depicted a guardian angel, hovering above a small boy and girl whose pursuit of a butterfly had brought them perilously close to a cliff's edge.

A framed photograph on the cabinet TV set caught my eye. It showed a pretty brown-skinned girl in academic cap and gown. Mrs. Fell saw me looking at it and said, with infinite pride in her voice, "My daughter. That was her high school graduation picture. She's a freshman at Southampton College now."

Her voice became matter of fact. "My charge is five dollars even if I don't get results, ten dollars if I do."

"All right."

She gestured toward a table covered with a printed cloth, near the front window. A pair of brown upholstered chairs with high backs and open wooden arms were drawn up on either side of it. On the table was a glass ball resting on a wooden stand. "We'll sit there."

When we were seated opposite each other I looked at the crystal ball and again felt humiliated that I, Diana Garson, had come to consult a woman who, more than likely, was a charlatan. She said, "Never mind the crystal. It's just to help me concentrate. It's in my mind that pictures form." A flicker of amusement in her dark eyes made me think that she had perceived the conflict between my need and my skepticism, between my desire for whatever help she could give me and my feeling that in seeking such help I violated my self-respect.

She said, "Do you want to tell me about it first?"

"It's—it's about some people named Woodhull, a mother and her grown son and daughter. They lived in this house near Quogsett that I've rented for the summer. Twenty-five years ago the power boat on which they were taking a cruise blew up. No trace of them was ever found. Maybe you remember the case."

"No. Twenty-five years ago I was fifteen and living with my folks in South Carolina." She paused. "Are you kin to those Woodhulls?"

"No. I never heard of them until a few weeks ago."

"Then how come you're interested in them?"

I told her all of it, starting with the first time I had sensed the presence of those three, and ending with the fire, and Mary Conski and the barrier her stolid presence seemed to keep in place.

Irene Fell's dark, enigmatic eyes studied me. "And what is it you want me to find out for you? What happened on that boat?"

"Yes." After a moment I burst out, "Perhaps then I'll be free of them."

Maybe it was because I was twenty-five miles from that house, but suddenly I realized just how desperately I wanted to be free of them. Yes, in spite of the strange content that just the sense of their presence in that house had brought me for days on end, and despite those moments, dreamlike and lovely in my memory, when I had seemed to see them, talk to them, touch them. For me they were like some seductive but dangerous drug. Even if David were not part of my life, even if I did not feel my chance of happiness with him was at stake, I still would have wanted to be free of those people from the sea.

The woman shook her head. "Maybe you won't feel free even if I can tell you what you want to know. But I'll try."

She did not make passes above the globe with her hands, like a medium in a film. Instead she sat with her hands curled loosely on the table and her gaze fixed on the ball. Minutes passed. I heard a catbird's rasping call, probably from the juniper bush I'd seen below the window, and cars passing along the street, and distant music from someone's radio or TV. Irene Fell still sat there, motionless except for her quiet breathing, with her gaze fixed on the globe.

Then, feeling a ripple down my spine, I saw the curled hands straighten out, stiffen. My gaze flew to her face. Her eyes, staring at the globe, were distended. Her breathing seemed to stop for a moment and then resume, more rapid now and quite audible.

I said, past the racing pulse in my throat, "What is it? What do you see?"

Not answering, she kept staring at the globe, horror in her eyes.

"What is it?" I cried again.

Her eyes closed and she slumped back into her chair. A shudder went through her body. Then she stayed motionless, knuckles gripping the chair arms. I watched her, too frightened now even to speak.

At last she opened her eyes. There was a lingering horror in their depths. Otherwise her face was expressionless. "You'll have to go now. I have things to tend to."

I said, dumfounded, "Go! But what did you see?"

Her dark gaze was direct now, and calm. "Nothing."

"But you did! You must have!"

"Girl, I told you. I saw nothing." She leaned forward. "But I do have one thing to say to you. Get out of that place. Go back to New York. Forget all this."

I was trembling with frustration and anger. "Why do you say that? Tell me! You've got to!"

Her speech, carefully northern until now, seemed to revert to her South Carolina childhood. "I doan have to do *nuthin'*, nuthin' you tell me to, leastways. I pay my taxes, and keep a neat place, and doan mess with big shots or any kind of heavy stuff." She stood up. "Go on, girl. Go back to New York."

I, too, got to my feet. "Five dollars, I believe you said?" Fumbling with the catch of my shoulder bag, I said bitterly, "I think you're a fraud. Now you'll say that for twenty-five dollars you'll tell me what you saw."

"Didn't you hear me?" Her northern manner of speech was back in place. "I told you I didn't see anything. And I don't want any money from you. Not five dollars, not one dollar, not five cents. And about my being a fraud, I don't care what you think. All I want is for you to leave so I can get on with the things I have to do."

Confused and angry and frightened, I turned and walked to the door.

Chapter 11

A few minutes later, as I drove down Riverhead's main street, I saw on a corner the glass-plated front of a General Motors agency, with a blue Dodge sedan revolving slowly on a circular platform inside. Was this one of Winstead Chalmers' showrooms? Probably. If I remembered correctly, Beth had said that her fiancé had the franchise for the entire East End. Probably Chalmers himself wasn't here in Riverhead, though. Beth had said that his Southampton office was his headquarters.

My thoughts returned to that frustrating session with Irene Fell. Was she just a clever charlatan? Did she count upon my returning tomorrow to offer her a hundred dollars or more? I didn't think so.

But if not a fraud, then she was certainly a liar. "I saw nothing," she said, when it appeared obvious from the horror in her eyes that she had seen something, or thought she had. But she wouldn't talk to me about it because she refused to "mess" with anything "heavy." What did she mean by "heavy"? The law? Important people? Or merely something so horrifying that she was determined not to discuss it?

Whatever the case, I was sure I could learn nothing from her. I would have to try some other way.

The sign for the turnoff to Southampton loomed up. I had a sudden impulse to see again that mansion on First Neck Lane where that old man lived, that man who had hated his first wife and who, incredibly, had said of his own flesh and blood, "I have no children."

A few minutes later I drove slowly along that street of large houses, standing far back behind thick hedges and brick or stone walls. There, just ahead, were those two stone gateposts set in the tall yew hedge. I drove even more slowly. As I passed the gateway, I looked in at the sprawling house and saw a long limousine parked at the foot of the broad front steps. Perhaps one— or both—of the Gregory Woodhulls was going for a drive. I continued on for a few yards and then stopped at the side of the road.

Not more than three minutes later, watching in the rearview mirror, I saw the limousine emerge from between the gateposts. My pulses quickened. As I had hoped, it was turning, not toward the center of the village, but toward me.

The big car, moving at a decorous thirty miles an hour, drove past. I saw Caroline Woodhull's startled face turn toward me. Then, a moment later, both her face and that of her aged husband appeared in the limousine's rear window. In the second or two that they looked back at me I caught the impression that they were not only indignant, but alarmed. I realized that a certain amount of paranoia became second nature to the rich. Did they think that my reappearance here meant that I was a scout for a burglary ring, or a reporter for some scandal sheet? Or did they have some other reason for being alarmed just by the sight of me?

Their faces disappeared. The car continued on for perhaps a hundred yards and then turned into a gateway. From my earlier visit to First Neck Lane, I knew that was the entrance to the Meadow Club.

I still sat there, thinking. Gregory Woodhull, confined to a wheelchair now, but twenty-five years ago perhaps a vigorous man of middle age—a man who wanted to marry again but found himself tied to a woman who, apparently, would not divorce him. And what of Caroline, the woman he had married after his wife's death? She must have been in her twenties back in those days. But no, it couldn't have been Caroline. Even though she still had the look of an athletic woman, with muscles hardened by tennis and swimming, I found it impossible to think of that patrician blonde guiding a small boat across black water, maneuvering it close to the hull of a power cruiser—

I started the car, made a U-turn in the empty street, and drove back to the main part of town.

Just beyond the village limits I again slowed. Ahead was the building that housed the Southampton dealership for General Motors cars. It was in a white brick building set back from the road. Smaller than its counterpart in Riverhead, it was far more attractive, with a graveled parking area and beds of pale yellow marigolds and scarlet sage along its plate-glass façade. Would Winstead Chalmers be there? The chances were excellent that he would. It was a quarter of three now, well past the lunch hour. I turned into the graveled space, stopped, and sat there for a while, rehearsing what I would say.

At last I went in. A blond young man, dapper in summer-weight red and white plaid slacks and red linen blazer, advanced smiling between the shiny cars standing on the yellow-tiled floor. "Good afternoon! What can I do for you?"

"I'd like to see Mr. Chalmers, please."

He hesitated, still smiling. "I'm afraid he's rather busy."

"Well, if he could possibly see me—" I added, "I'm a friend of Miss Warren's."

"Oh, in that case I'm sure he'll see you. What is your name, please?"

I told him, and then followed him across the room to a door set in the rear wall. "Miss Garson to see you, Mr. Chalmers." I stepped inside, and the salesman closed the door behind me.

Winstead Chalmers didn't look busy. His feet were resting on his desk, and he held a copy of *Sports Illustrated*. Hastily he took his feet down, laid the magazine on the desk, and stood up. For a moment he looked puzzled. Then he said, "Oh, yes. You were having lunch with Beth one day at the Road Race. Sit down, Miss Garson, sit down."

I took the chair opposite him. When we were both seated, he said, "What brings you here?"

"I'm thinking of buying a car, an inexpensive one."

"Then you've come to the right place. We think our low-priced models are the best values the industry is turning out these days."

"I'd heard that if you shop around among the agencies—"

"You can get a better deal? You certainly can. And since you're a friend of Beth's maybe we can sweeten the deal even more. I suppose you have a car to turn in."

"No, I'm driving a rented VW."

"Too bad," he said, and then added, with the air of a man who never knocks any kind of competition, "Not that renting doesn't make sense under certain circumstances. But buying a car is just as cheap in the long run, and besides you have the pride of ownership. Do you have any particular make in mind?"

"Not really."

"Well, let's go look around a little."

Out in the showroom he led me to a canary-yellow car, a small Buick. For several minutes he talked of superior mileage and roadability and ease of parking. Uncomfortable with my deception, and anxious to get to the point of my visit, I scarcely listened.

"Now let's look at the engine." He walked to the front of the car and raised the hood.

I said swiftly, "You know, Mr. Chalmers, you haven't changed much."

For a moment he looked disconcerted. Then he laughed. "You mean, since we met two or three weeks ago? I should hope not."

"I mean since twenty-five years ago."

He stared at me. "Twenty-five years ago! Why, you weren't even alive then."

"I was about a year old. But it's from a photograph of you that I know how you looked then."

"Photograph? Where did you see a photograph of me?"

"It was a snapshot in this album I found in the house I've rented for the summer. Did Beth tell you that I rented the house where a Mrs. Woodhull and her son and daughter lived?"

He was not smiling now. After a moment he said curtly, "No."

"Well, I did. And I found this album with a lot of old snapshots of the family and a few other people and of the boat Derek

Woodhull had, the one that burned and went down with him and his mother and sister aboard. You were in a snapshot with Sheila Woodhull. I knew it was you because Mrs. Woodhull had written beneath each snapshot, naming the people in it."

For a long moment he looked at me, his face cold now and a little pale under its tan, giving him a muddy look. "Very interesting," he said finally. He looked at his watch. "You'll have to excuse me now. I've just remembered that I'm expecting an important phone call. I'll let our Mr. Johannsen explain the engine to you."

"Don't bother. I probably wouldn't understand much about the engine. And you've given me a lot of information. I'll think it over, and make up my mind. Good-bye, Mr. Chalmers."

He closed the hood with what seemed to me more force than necessary. "Good-bye, Miss Garson."

I went out to the VW and turned it onto the highway. As I drove slowly toward Quogsett I wondered what it was that had caused him to lose color. Was it the reminder of a long-ago humiliation and pain that Sheila Woodhull had inflicted upon him? Perhaps. Perhaps the hurt had gone very deep, so deep that until just recently he had not asked any other woman to marry him. Certainly Beth Warren had not mentioned any previous marriage of his.

Beth. Could she be the reason for his reaction? According to Beth herself, he hated to be reminded that his future wife was the child befriended one long-ago summer by the Woodhulls, a child who didn't even know who had fathered her.

Well, one thing was certain. If he told Beth Warren of my visit, and I was almost certain he'd do so, she would be very angry indeed.

Chapter 12

I was in the dining room the next morning, eating the last of my scrambled eggs and toast, when the phone rang. I went into the living room and lifted the phone from its cradle. "Hello."

Beth said coldly, "What the hell did you think you were doing yesterday?"

I remained silent. There was no point in trying to pretend that I didn't know her meaning.

"Don't you remember my telling you specifically that I didn't want Win Chalmers to be reminded of—of all that old stuff?"

I said nothing, because I was sure she already knew the answer. She had driven David to the station that morning. And he, in his worry and frustration, must have told her what I had said about my obsessive need to find out what had happened to the Woodhulls.

Beth said, into the silence, "I wish to hell Doris Gowrey had kicked you out when she had the chance."

I blurted out, almost involuntarily, "Beth, did you start that incinerator fire?"

She answered slowly, in the tone of one shaking her head, "You really are crazy, aren't you?"

"Perhaps. All I know is that I didn't start that fire, and yet it nearly got me evicted from this house."

"Which you should have been. But instead you blackmailed

poor old Doris into letting you stay, with only that halfwit Mary Conski to see that you don't start more fires or do something equally crazy." After a moment she added abruptly, "I guess there's no point in continuing this conversation."

She hung up. I did, too, and then stood motionless for a moment. Would she phone or visit Doris Gowrey now and try to persuade her to evict me, after all? I hoped not. There was something I needed to know from Doris Gowrey, and if she were angry with me it would be just that much harder to get her to talk.

Swiftly I went upstairs to get my handbag. As I passed Mary Conski's room I heard the murmur of her radio from behind the closed door.

According to the phone book, Miss Gowrey lived at Two-twelve Chilton, one of the streets running west off Main Street. I drove slowly past modest turn-of-the-century frame houses, which, with their bay windows and porch swings and hydrangea bushes, looked like a set for those old Andy Hardy movies. Number Two-twelve was smaller than the other houses, a one-story clapboard bungalow. Its yellow paint was dingy, and the lawn needed cutting. As I went up the overgrown flagstone walk I felt a pang of compunction. Perhaps she did badly need the income from that house beside the dune, and if so, she had every reason to worry that someone might start rumors that would make it hard to rent.

Standing on the tiny porch, I pressed the doorbell and heard a harsh ringing inside. After a few seconds she opened the door. The leap of surprise in her face made me think that as yet Beth had not been in touch with her.

"May I talk to you for a few minutes, Miss Gowrey? It's about Gregory Woodhull."

I saw hostility and curiosity warring in her face. Curiosity won. She opened the door a little wider and said in a grudging tone, "Come in."

The living room was small. There was a TV set on a rollaway stand, a sagging black sofa of what looked like genuine leather, and two armchairs, one with worn electric-blue upholstery and the other wearing a ready-made knitted slipcover of green and brown checks. There were several small tables. It was the sort of room where you would expect to see family photographs covering every available surface. There were no photographs.

She waved a hand toward the blue armchair and said, still in that grudging tone, "Sit down."

She herself sank into the other armchair. "Now what's this about Gregory Woodhull?"

Her directness disconcerted me momentarily. Then I said, "The first time I saw you, it seemed to me that—that you implied that Mrs. Woodhull—the first Mrs. Woodhull, I mean—wasn't faithful to her husband."

For a moment she was silent. I could see another struggle in her face now, one between her hostility toward me and her desire to talk about the sister she'd hated and envied. Then she said, with a rush, "Did I? I don't remember. But if I did, I don't mind repeating it, because it's true. Now what did you have to tell me about Gregory?"

"I went to see him right after I found that album. He wouldn't take it. I said something about its containing pictures of his children, and he said something very strange. He said, 'I had no son and daughter.' At the time I thought he just meant that they'd displeased him to the point where he'd refused to acknowledge them. But yesterday I caught a glimpse of him and his present wife, and I got to thinking—"

"That maybe he meant exactly what he said? He did, and it's true. Derek and Sheila weren't his children."

I said, after a long moment, "Then why didn't he divorce her? Why did he consent to just a separation?"

"Because he didn't know the truth until just a short time before Grace and the children died in that accident."

"How did—"

"He went to his doctor for a complete checkup. I guess he was in love with Caroline—Caroline Tate, her name was—even then, although I didn't know that." An old bitterness made the lines in her face look even deeper. "And I guess he had some hope he could bribe Grace into setting him free. Anyway, he asked the doctor to find out if he could still become a father. The tests showed he was sterile, and probably always had been."

I said, after a shocked moment, "You mean his doctor told people—"

"Not the doctor. The doctor's nurse. Not a trained nurse, just a kind of office assistant. She told people, and I guess it got back to Gregory."

I said, puzzled, "But why didn't he demand a divorce then? He had the grounds."

"Maybe he did plan to sue for divorce. Maybe not. I guess if Grace had fought it, it would have been a very messy case, so messy that Caroline might have refused to marry him. After all, she was beautiful and came from a good family. She had plenty of other offers. As it turned out, there was no need for a divorce. Grace died on that boat."

She didn't add, as she had the last time I saw her, "And I'm alive and still going strong." But her tone, sourly triumphant, implied the words.

I said, "About Derek and Sheila. Do you know—"

"Who their father was? I know. Sheila even looked like him, and Derek did a little, even though he was dark like his mother. Their father was Travis Eaton, the man Grace was in love with when she married Gregory on the rebound. For several years after she married Gregory she used to go into New York every few weeks or so and meet Travis. They'd go to a hotel just off Washington Square. The hotel isn't there anymore.

"If you're wondering how I know," she went on, "it was because I made it my business to find out. I went to New York myself and hired a private detective. He sent me regular reports."

I felt pity and revulsion at the thought of her in those days, so eaten up with envy and thwarted passion that she'd hired a man to spy on her own sister.

"I should have thought," I said, in as neutral a tone as possible, "that you would have shown the reports to Gregory."

"That was the last thing I wanted to do. Oh, he might have divorced her, but he'd have disliked me from then on for being the one who handed him the evidence. I kept hoping he'd find out some other way that Grace was unfaithful. But he didn't, not until it was too late, not until Caroline Tate was in the picture—"

She broke off and then demanded, eyes brilliant behind her

glasses, "Why did you come here and get me talking about things that are none of your business?"

When I didn't answer, she said, "Are you just nosy? Is that it?"

"Perhaps. But naturally what Gregory Woodhull said about having no children made me wonder—"

"At your age, you shouldn't be wondering what happened in other people's lives donkey's years ago. You should be getting on with your own life."

My own life. If only she knew how much I wanted to get on with it.

She still stared at me, questions in the bright gray eyes behind the glasses. I braced myself to meet them. But all she said was, "How are you getting along with Mary Conski?"

"All right. We don't see much of each other. In fact, I scarcely know she's there." Except, of course, for that barrier her stolid presence seemed to erect.

I went on, "I'm sorry about coming here to ask you questions about Gregory Woodhull."

"Well, maybe it was good for me for once not to keep everything bottled up. You see, most of my friends are gone now, and even when they were alive, nobody seemed much interested. Interested in how my life was ruined, I mean, when Grace—"

She broke off, and then said, "But maybe you'd better excuse me now, Miss Garson. I'm expecting a mason to fix the bedroom ceiling, and I want to get the furniture covered up before he lets plaster dust fall all over it."

Out in the VW once more, I drove slowly toward Main Street. I was a little less worried about Beth Warren now. True, she still might try to get Doris Gowrey to make another eviction attempt, but I was less afraid now that Beth would succeed. Perhaps I was wrong, but it seemed to me that my landlady, with no one else to talk to about her unhappy past, had been feeling almost friendly toward me by the time we said good-bye.

But that might change after Beth had talked to her. It would still be wise for me to gather as much knowledge as I could as soon as I could. And Lieutenant Larry Philbeam, who had served with Captain Derek Woodhull in Korea, might prove to be a likely source.

Chapter 13

I parked on Main Street, went into a drugstore, and consulted the directory dangling outside the phone booth. There was no listing for a Larry Philbeam. Well, no matter. I remembered the address given in that newspaper article about his arrest: Widow Winthrop's Path, Springs. I could find his house. But first I had to get the album.

I drove back to the house beside the dune. Mary Conski sat on the porch, rocking. As I went up the steps I greeted her, and she nodded, with no change of expression. In the living room I took the album from where I'd placed it in the bookcase. "So long," I said to Mary Conski as I started down the porch steps. She nodded.

I drove back to East Hampton, continued on to its northern outskirts, and then took the road to Springs, a two-lane road bordered by trees and scattered houses, some of recent construction but many both old and small. After about ten minutes I saw, facing me along a road that ran at right angles to the one I was on, a frame structure labeled "General Store." That, apparently, was Springs' entire business district. I went inside and asked a middle-aged man who stood behind a counter if he knew how I could find Widow Winthrop's Path.

"Sure." He drew a map from beneath the counter and unfolded it. "Here we are. You'll have to go back toward East

Hampton a couple of miles. See, here it is snaking off to your right through the woods. You'll have to keep a sharp lookout for the entrance to it. Those back roads are pretty narrow." He paused. "Social worker?"

"No," I said.

"Thought you might be."

"No," I said again. I thanked him and went out to my car.

A few minutes later, as I drove slowly along the two-lane road, I saw a weathered sign marking the entrance to the even narrower Widow Winthrop's Path. At first, as I drove over its uneven surface, I saw nothing but trees on either side. Then I began to see small houses, some separated by a hundred yards or so, others closely grouped. A few of the little houses were very old, perhaps dating from Colonial times. Had one of them, I wondered, been Widow Winthrop's house? Most of the houses, though, could have been thrown together from scrap lumber, tar paper, and flattened tin cans at almost any time in the past, including last week. And no matter what the age of materials of the houses, all had roofs in need of repair. All of the front yards were either weed grown or completely bare, littered with rusting cars and noisy with squawking, scratching chickens.

As I drove along, I kept watching for someone from whom I might ask directions. At last I saw in one of the bare front yards a thin blond woman of about thirty-five, with a man's blue shirt hanging loose over her chinos. She was throwing grain to a small flock of Plymouth Rock hens. A towheaded little girl stood nearby, thumb in her mouth. I turned into the yard and stopped.

"Could you tell me where Larry Philbeam lives?"

"Sure could." Her smile was friendly. "You from the Relief?"

"No." I could see how both the man in the store and this woman should think I might be a case worker. Widow Winthrop's Path appeared to be a dwelling place of the indolent, the inept, or the merely unlucky.

"I thought you might have come to investigate them. Lord knows they ought to be." Her smile had gone. "Not that I think it's any disgrace to be on relief, understand. We had to go on it. My husband—he was a roofer—got hurt so bad in a fall that he has to stay in bed most of the time. And we got three kids, this one and two older ones. But this Larry Philbeam and his woman, nothing wrong with them except booze." She broke off, looking aghast. "You're not a relative, are you?"

"No."

"You never can tell. All kinds of Philbeams out here on the East End."

"So I've heard."

"Matter of fact, Larry's own father was one of the high-up Philbeams. Owned a horse farm. And they say Larry himself was once an officer. In the army, I mean. Nobody'd ever think it now."

"Did you say you know where he lives?"

"'Bout a half mile from here, on your left. Little tiny shack. Most of the time his car is out front. An old green Dodge."

I thanked her and left.

I had no trouble finding the place. The green Dodge, liberally dented, stood in the front yard. So did two rusty wrecks, stripped of their headlights and tires. The house, about the size of a two-car garage, had been covered with tar paper, but in spots the tar paper had peeled off, showing the bare knotted boards underneath. I parked beside the Dodge, picked up the album from the car seat, and went to the door.

For a moment after I knocked there was silence. Then I heard a stumbling sound and a crash. I also became aware that someone inside the house was snoring.

The door opened, and a woman of about the same age as the one I'd just talked to looked out at me. This one, though, was a brunette, and about twenty pounds overweight. She wore a rumpled brown blouse with yellow poppies on it, and white shorts that revealed purplish bruises on her plump white legs. Another bruise, faded to green, surrounded her left eye. She had been drinking. I could smell it.

I said, aware that the snoring sound was louder now that the door stood open, "My name is Diana Garson. I wonder if I might see Mr. Larry Philbeam."

Her rather prominent brown eyes went from my face to the album and back to my face. Their expression was both interested and suspicious. "You selling something?"

"No. But I found this old album in the house I rented for the summer and there's a picture of Mr. Philbeam in it, in uniform. I thought he might be interested in seeing it."

"No kidding! An old picture of Larry? Let's see it."

I opened the album and leafed through it until I found the snapshots taken in Korea. "There he is," I said, handing her the album. "And there's another picture, and another. Mrs. Woodhull—this album was hers—wrote Mr. Philbeam's name and her son's under each of the snapshots."

She laughed. "So that's what Larry looked like in those days. Who'da thunk it?"

"This album has gotten me interested in the Woodhulls. Mrs. Woodhull and her son and daughter are all dead, of course."

She was still looking at the snapshots. "No kidding? All three?"

"Yes. They died in a boating accident about twenty-five years ago. Didn't you know about it?"

"How could I?" she said, with a touch of indignation. "Twenty-five years ago I was practically in my cradle. Besides, I'm not from around here. I was raised in Riverhead."

"I thought, Mr. Philbeam might have told you about it."

"He talked some about the guy who's in these pictures with him." Squinting slightly, she reread a caption. "Yeah, Derek Woodhull. He told me about him. But he never mentioned a boat accident."

"Perhaps if I could see him—"

Again she laughed, and handed the album back to me. "You can see him, but he can't see you. He's blind. Blind drunk, that is." She opened the door wider. "But come on in."

I stepped over the sill. There was another door, I saw now, in the far wall. It stood partly open, and the snores came from beyond it.

She righted a straight chair, which, apparently, she'd upset on her way to answer my knock. She closed the front door and then walked to a TV set in one corner of the room. A McDonald's commercial was on the small screen. What with her voice and mine and the snoring, I hadn't been aware of the sound of the

TV. She flipped a switch. The capering figures on the screen were replaced by a dwindling dot of light.

She turned to me, eyes bright with malice. "You want to see what he looks like now?"

I said, disconcerted, "Oh, no! I don't want to disturb him."

"The only way you could disturb him is with an axe. Come on."

Reluctant, but fascinated, I followed her to the partially opened door. She opened it wider. A man lay on his back atop the pink chenille spread on a sagging double bed. He wore a white shirt and stained khaki pants but no shoes or socks. He had loosened the buckle of the belt that surrounded a girth of perhaps fifty inches. His eyes were partially open and his mouth, surrounded by gray stubble, was open wide, emitting those raucous sounds. The only discernible resemblance between him and the thin young lieutenant of the snapshots was that they were both human and both male.

I backed into the outer room and she closed the door. "Sit down," she said, "sit down."

I took one of the two straight chairs. They stood on either side of the table, which held several empty glasses, a bottle of bourbon about half full, and two of the metal trays in which frozen dinners come, each tray with a little mashed potatoes and gravy left in it. There were no other chairs. On one side of the room stood a fairly new-looking gas stove, a sink, and a small refrigerator. Evidently there was a cat somewhere about the premises because on the floor near the sink was a red plastic bowl, half filled with some soft-looking food, with the word "Kitty" printed in white on its side. Flies were helping themselves to the food Kitty had left.

My hostess said, "How about a drinkee?"

Because I felt I needed to keep all my wits about me, I'd prepared myself, as soon as I saw the bourbon bottle, to meet that suggestion. "I can't. I've taken some antihayfever pills, and they don't mix with alcohol, you know. But please don't let that stop you." I laid the album in front of me on the table.

"Well, if you're sure you don't mind." She poured bourbon into a glass, took it to the sink, and added water from the tap.

When she came back and sat down I said, in a low voice, "You mentioned that—"

"You don't have to whisper. He can't hear us when he's snoring like that." She took a long swallow of her drink.

"All right, Mrs. Philbeam. You mentioned that—"

"I'm not Mrs. Philbeam," she said scornfully. "My name is Bernice Hays, *Miss* Hays. Only they call me Birdie. You think I'd marry someone like that, when I've been a model and all?"

I didn't say anything, and I hoped my expression didn't either.

"There used to be this department store in Riverhead, see? They had a coffee shop where the customers could get a bite to eat and see some of the salesgirls model the store's dresses. I was one of the ones they picked to model. I was kind of plump even then, so I modeled their line of dresses and housecoats called Pretty Plenty. Then about eight years ago I got sick and lost my job, and before I started to look for another one I met Larry, and one thing led to another, and finally I moved in here.

"But I'm not going to stay," she went on broodingly. "Why should I stay with a man who beats on me? As soon as this last shiner he gave me goes away I'm going to leave. I'm going to get a waitress job, and lose a few pounds, and then go back to modeling. And not in a hick town like Riverhead, either! I'm going to New York."

I had a depressed feeling that she had made this same speech again and again over the last eight years, both to herself and to him, and would make it again in the years ahead.

"You mentioned that your—that Mr. Philbeam sometimes talks of Derek Woodhull."

Again malice brightened her face. "Yeah, but only when he's drunk, so drunk I'm sure he don't remember afterward. You know what that snoring tub of lard did in Korea? He tried to desert to the Gooks. You know, the North Koreans, only he tells me the Chinese were in on it, too, by that time. Anyway, he was in this squad where Derek was captain. Or do I mean squad?"

"I think it's called a company if there's a captain in charge of it."

"Whatever." She took another long swallow. "Anyway, they'd had it rough, see? It was winter and they were retreating and they'd lost a lot of men. One night Larry decided he'd had enough. He tried to crawl off to where the Gooks were and give himself up. But this friend of his, this Dirk Woodhull—or was it Dirk?"

"Derek."

"This Derek, being a friend of his since they were both kids, he must have guessed Larry was about to crack, because he followed him and caught up with him. The damn fool even had a stick with a white handkerchief tied to it, all ready to wave."

I said, after a long moment, "And Derek didn't report him?"

"No, I guess he couldn't stand the thought of the damn fool getting shot, even though I guess this Derek would of got shot, too, if they found out how he covered up. Anyway, he took Larry back to camp, and Larry was a good boy from then on, and finally they both came home. Maybe everything would have been all right for Larry if some friend of the family hadn't wangled a job for him down in Washington, in the States Department."

"The States—? Oh, yes, the State Department."

"That's right. It wasn't a big job, no secrets attached to it or anything, but after a few months Larry got ambitious and applied for a bigger job, I guess the kind of job where there would be secrets. They had to investigate before they gave it to him, of course, so they came to his old captain."

"And Derek told them about what had happened in Korea?"

"He told them. I guess keeping a friend from getting shot was one thing. But letting a guy like Larry take a job where he might learn things, big things, that he shouldn't give away— Well, that was something else. They couldn't give him one of those military trials, not when he was out of the army, but he got fired, of course, with no chance to ever get another government job. In fact, I guess that States Department job was the last one he ever held for more than a few weeks. And I guess he finally decided that work interfered with his drinking, so he gave it up. Work, I mean."

After a while I said, "He must have felt bitter toward Derek Woodhull."

"Bitter! The names he's called his old buddy would curl the quills on a porcupine."

"But he's never said anything about the boat accident?"

"What boat accident? Oh yes, you told me. The one that killed this Derek and his mother and sister. No, all he's told me is that the lousy stool pigeon—only he didn't say lousy—has been dead for years."

"Doesn't it seem strange to you that he never mentioned how Derek Woodhull died?"

"Strange?" She leaned toward me, her eyes suddenly bright. "You mean, maybe Larry got even. Maybe he did something to—"

That inner door banged against the wall. Larry Philbeam stood there, his big body nearly filling the doorway, one hand braced against the frame. My heart gave an almost painful leap. When had he waked up? Whenever it was, I had been too intent upon Birdie's words—and she probably had been too drunk—to notice that the snoring had stopped.

He looked at Birdie. "You bitch." His light-blue eyes, bloodshot and enraged, appeared small in his puffy face. "Been blabbing, have you?"

Instinctively I reached out and grasped the album. His eye swung to me. "And who the hell are you? Snooping around here—"

He took a stumbling step toward me. Birdie shot up from her chair and grasped his thick right arm with both hands. "Run!" she shrieked. "I can handle him. Run!"

He still moved toward me, dragging her with him. My temporary paralysis left me. I got up and bolted, the album clutched in my left hand. I opened the door with my right and plunged down the single step to the hard-packed yard. Behind me I heard a crash. Perhaps he'd stumbled over his own feet, or perhaps she had thrown a chair in his way. I kept going. I threw the album onto the VW's front seat, got in after it, and turned the key. The little car bucked forward.

I saw in the rearview mirror that he was out of the house by then, and running after me. As I turned onto the road I saw him change direction and head for the green Dodge. I'd gone only a few yards when, looking into the mirror, I saw the Dodge turn onto the road. Heart pounding, hands sweaty on the wheel, I pressed harder on the accelerator.

The road was narrow and winding. I dared not drive too fast lest I shoot off among the trees. Old as his car was, it was more powerful than mine, and besides, he undoubtedly knew each curve of the road. Mouth dry with fear at the thought of those big fists pummeling me, I saw that he was gaining on me every second.

A few yards ahead, that blond woman who had given me directions was still in her yard. Should I turn in there? No. What good would another woman and her bedridden husband be against a violent and drunken man? Better to pray I could get to the highway, where some motorist might help me.

When I finally turned onto the two-laned paved road, he was only about twenty yards behind me. He, too, made the turn. I pressed the accelerator down to the floorboard. With despair I saw that there were no visible cars traveling in either direction. And even though the old Dodge was swaying, now on one side of the white line and now on the other, he still gained on me.

I turned a curve. Ahead was a panel truck, coming from the other direction. Evidently Larry Philbeam saw it, too, and spun his steering wheel sharply to get back on the right side of the line. In the mirror I saw the old car shoot off the road. Then I heard a crash.

I drove to the roadside, stopped, and turned to look through the rear window. The Dodge's rear wheels were barely off the road, and its nose was jammed against a tree trunk. Should I go back there? He might be badly injured, even dead. And there was no other car in sight, not even the panel truck.

As I hesitated, the Dodge's door opened. Larry Philbeam got out and stood there swaying, his hand still on the door handle. I drove off.

A few minutes later I came to the first of a cluster of small houses. An elderly man was mowing the scrap of lawn with an old push-pull mower. I stopped and said, "Excuse me, but a car's piled into a tree about a mile back there. Would you mind phoning the police about it?"

"Sure thing," he said, and hurried toward his front door. I drove on. Perhaps, I reflected, I should talk to the police myself and make a charge against Larry Philbeam. But what sort of charge? Assault? He hadn't assaulted me. He hadn't even caught up with me. Besides, I fervently hoped that after he sobered up he would remember little or nothing of my conversation with Birdie. And if I went to the police they would want to know the reason for my visit to that tar-paper shack. They would question both Larry and Birdie, and soon, no matter how little he actually remembered of my visit, he would gain some idea of why I had come to his house. He would not take kindly to the thought of anyone raking up that old business in Korea.

If it did turn out that he did not remember my visit, there would be little chance of Birdie telling him about it. She had every reason to know what would happen if she did. He would beat her up first, and then come looking for me.

As I drove down East Hampton's lovely Main Street, I glanced at my watch and saw, with surprise, that it was not yet noon.

Chapter 14

When I reached the house beside the dune, Mary Conski no longer sat on the front porch, nor did I see her inside the house, although I could hear the murmur of her radio in her room. I prepared and ate a sketchy lunch. The day had turned cloudy and cool by then, too cool for swimming, but not too cool for sitting on the sand. I climbed the stairs, changed to shorts and a sweater in my room, and then left the house.

Because of the weather, the beach on the other side of the dune was empty except for a few hardy souls—a group of teen-agers tossing a Frisbee and a couple of surf fishermen in waders. I sat there looking out over the gray water. In my mind's eye, though, I was seeing a black Atlantic and a child floating in it, a child who had babbled to her rescuers about a figure stepping over a power boat's railing. Not for the first time, I wondered if that story, despite her later contradiction of it, could have been true. In that case, could Larry Philbeam have been the boat's invader? Certainly he had reason to hate Derek Woodhull. He must have felt—must still feel, in self-justifying moments—that Derek had ruined his life.

But would even a Larry Philbeam have been willing to set fire to a boat when there were other people, including a ten-year-old girl, aboard it? Perhaps. He was not only a violent man, but a cowardly and treacherous one. An officer, he'd tried to slip away from his hard-pressed comrades in the hope of saving his own skin. And if he'd succeeded in surrendering to an enemy patrol, he probably wouldn't have hesitated to give every scrap of military information he had in the hope of getting good treatment, no matter how many lives that information might cost.

I sat on the beach until midafternoon and then went back to the house. I took the old vacuum cleaner from its cubbyhole under the stairs and set to work, sweeping the hall and dining room and living room. After that I dusted and washed smudged areas on the walls around the light switches. Although Mrs. Conski took care of her own room and was meticulous about leaving the kitchen neat after her solitary meals, she seemed averse to helping out in other parts of the house. I could understand such an aversion. Until she hurt her back, she must have spent most of the days of her life cleaning other people's houses.

I had finished my labors and was immersed in a heavy-breathing novel by Ouida, when the phone rang. "Hi, kiddo!" It was Birdie's voice. She sounded very chipper indeed. "I remembered your first name because I've always liked it, and your last name because it's the same as that old movie star's, so I called information and got your number."

She sounded proud of herself for remembering. Evidently she was in some café or bar, because in the background I could hear voices mingling with a Dolly Parton recording. "I just wanted you to know you got nothing to worry about. He don't remember a thing."

"Good," I said with sincere fervor. "Where is he now?"

"Back at the house, snoring again. As I guess maybe you know, he piled into a tree. The cops picked him up for drunk driving, and then another cop came to tell me about it. Well, I had some money in the old sock—I always go through his pockets when he's really stinko—so I asked some pals of ours to drive me to the station to bail him out. I'm still with them."

I thought wonderingly, why? Why had she bailed out that repulsive creature who regularly, in her phrase, beat on her? The way of a man with a maid, and vice versa, was not only a thing full of wonder, as the Bible said. Sometimes it was downright ridiculous.

"Well, Diana, I just wanted you to know everything's okey-dokey. He'll never know anything from me, or anybody else, because I'm not telling anybody."

"Thanks, Birdie, more than I can say. And good luck."

"So long," she said, and hung up.

I did, too, and then stood there with my hand on the phone. Somehow I trusted Birdie, but I didn't trust Larry Philbeam at all. If he did remember, he'd be sly enough to try to hide that fact.

I thrust the worry from my mind. Birdie knew him very well, so well that it was unlikely that he could fool her. If she said he'd forgotten, then he'd forgotten. I went back to the kitchen. It was empty. Mrs. Conski had finished her last meal of the day. I set about preparing my own.

Two nights later, as I was carrying the plates I'd used at dinner back to the kitchen, the phone rang again. I set the plates down on the sinkboard and went back along the hall to the living room.

It was Beth Warren calling. She said, "How did you like Widow Winthrop's Path?"

After a surprised moment, I said, "How did you know about that?"

"Kelly Davis. He runs the general store in Springs. Kelly and I have an arrangement. When summer people looking for a place in Springs tell him they can't find one, he suggests they try Beth Warren's agency over in Quogsett. If the deal clicks, I pay him a little commission."

She paused. I waited in silence until she went on. "Kelly likes to talk about how foolhardy some of the summer people are—leaving their keys in their cars, swimming at night beyond the last line of breakers, and so on. When he called me today he said, 'There was this girl in here the other day, good looking and well dressed, wanting to know where Widow Winthrop's Path was. I figured maybe she was a social worker and would know what to do if one of those trashy characters back there in the woods jumped into her car, but she said no, she wasn't.'"

Again Beth paused, as if hoping I would speak, and again I said nothing. After a moment she went on, "I asked Kelly to describe the girl more specifically, and he said she was about five-feet-four, with dark hair and gray eyes, and that she was driving a green VW."

"And so?" I asked coldly.

"And so just this. I remember your asking me about Larry Philbeam after you'd seen an item in the *Star* about his umpteenth arrest. He lives on Widow Winthrop's Path. In fact, I know that a couple of hours after you asked directions at Kelly's store, Larry Philbeam piled up against a tree not far from the entrance to Widow Winthrop's Path."

I said nothing.

"What happened? Was he chasing you away from his place when he ran into that tree?"

"I don't have to answer a question like that."

She said, as if I hadn't spoken, "What were you doing over there, anyway? Did those three spooks of yours send you over to snoop around?"

So I had been correct in assuming that David, on the way to the station, had told her what I had confided to him the night before. No doubt he'd added, "For God's sake, Beth, think of some way of getting her out of that house." Even though I knew David had been acting for what he thought was my own good, I could not help feeling a flare of resentment.

I said, "I don't have to answer that question, either."

Again she ignored my words. "If your spooks did tell you to do it, they're giving you some bad advice. Summer people think that the Hamptons are all beaches and posh restaurants and quaint old houses. But there are some tough characters living on the back roads around here. Larry Philbeam is one of them. And if he decides to repay your visit, I don't think you'll find Mary Conski much protection."

So that was the point of her call. She was hoping that she could use the threat of Larry Philbeam to make me leave this house.

"You and Mary getting along all right?"

"We are."

"Just the same, wouldn't you like to consider that little house I mentioned just off Main Street in East Hampton? It's still available, and it's a darling house, and safe, with neighbors on both sides."

"No, thanks. I like it here."

"Well, it's your— No, I won't say it's your funeral. I'll just say it's your decision. I've got a dinner date, so I'll hang up now."

Perhaps it was her call, with its derisive reference to those shadowy three, that caused the dream I had that night, or rather, early the next morning.

In the dream I stood in half-darkness on a desolate plain. I have a feeling that it was a place I had seen only in photographs, the barren upland where Stonehenge stands. The Woodhulls were there, Mrs. Woodhull on my right, Derek on my left, and Sheila facing me. None of them was smiling.

Sheila said, "We're depending on you."

My dreaming self nodded, knowing what they meant. They depended upon me to reveal murder, to see that murder was punished.

Abruptly I awoke to gray light and sat up in bed. The atmosphere of the house had not changed. I still had the sense of a barrier separating me from those three who had appeared in my dream.

I became aware of a dripping sound outside the window. Rain? I turned my head. No, it was fog, dimly luminescent in the dawn light, pressing close to the window screen. I knew I could not get back to sleep. I dressed, went down to the kitchen, and managed to prepare a breakfast of coffee, orange juice, and toast and carry it into the dining room before I heard Mrs. Conski descending for her own breakfast.

A few hours later, in the living room, with the lamps on even though it was not yet eleven in the morning, I tried to follow Ouida's marathon sentences. I found it tough going. I felt too oppressed to concentrate, oppressed by the memory of my dream, by the lack of sufficient sleep, and by the windless fog that now was so thick that from the front window I could not even see the road, let alone the potato fields beyond it.

The phone rang, making me jump. I laid the book aside and went to answer it.

David said, "I'm coming down for the weekend."

"Weekend? You mean it's Friday?" I had a feeling that I'd said much the same thing the last time he had phoned to say he was coming out to the Hamptons.

"Yes, it's Friday."

"No."

"What do you mean, no?"

"I mean, don't come out here."

After several seconds he said, in a tone that made my heart contract, "Don't you want to see me, Diana?"

The words came before I could stop them. "I want to see you desperately."

"Then why—"

"I don't want to see you yet, and I don't want to see you here."

"Then come back to New York. God, how I hate passing the door of that empty apartment every night and morning." He essayed a small joke. "If you have to look at the ocean, you can ride the subway to Rockaway Beach every day for the rest of the summer."

"You know that's not why I'm staying. I told you why, the last time you were here. I'm staying because I feel I have to. I feel—"

"I remember what you said. You're swimming a river, and you have to keep trying to get to the other shore, because if you turn back now you'll drown." He paused, and then said, "Diana, I know that doctor at the clinic said you were fundamentally okay. But maybe, since you've been in that house—"

"I know. Maybe now I'm not okay. But I'm still going to stay here."

He was silent for so long that I began to fear he had hung up. I cried, "David!"

"Yes, I'm here."

"David, don't—don't forget me."

He gave a totally unamused laugh. "I sure as hell would if I could. But don't worry. I won't forget you. Okay, I won't come out there for the weekend. I ought to hole up to do some work, anyway. I'll keep in touch. Good-bye for now, Diana."

"Good-bye."

I went upstairs then and scrubbed the bathroom, even the

wall tiling that extended halfway to the ceiling. After time out for lunch, I went back upstairs, swept and dusted in my bedroom, the unoccupied bedroom, and the hall, and finally took down the curtains in both bedrooms. Even though I knew they would not dry in this weather, I took them downstairs to the laundry tubs on the screened back porch and washed them. Then I carried them through the thick fog to the clothesline that ran between a corner of the house and the garage. They would dry quickly once the fog lifted, if it ever did.

When I had placed the last clothespin, I just stood there, reluctant to go into the house. I could think of no more household tasks to occupy me, and I felt too keyed up to concentrate on a book.

Through the thick smother I heard what seemed to be the sound of an approaching car. The sound grew louder and then abruptly ceased, as if the car had stopped only a hundred feet or so away. But that couldn't be. Fog, I knew, distorted sound, making nearby noises seem distant and distant ones close. If the car had been as close as it sounded, I would have seen at least the dim loom of its headlights. Surely anyone rash enough to drive around in this pea soup wouldn't compound his folly by traveling without lights.

The thought, though, made me want to get in the VW and drive and drive, in the hope of outrunning this sense of oppression. I couldn't do that, of course, but at least I could walk.

After I entered the lighted back porch I looked at my watch. Almost five. I had best take my walk right away, before the day grew even darker. In the kitchen, bathed by the droplight's glare, Mary Conski stood at the sinkboard slicing a Polish sausage for dinner. I said, "Hello, there. This fog has made me restless. I think I'll go for a walk."

She nodded.

In a drawer of the kitchen cabinet was a large and comparatively new flashlight, no doubt left there by some forgetful former tenant. Carrying the flashlight, I went upstairs. Because I knew it would be chilly at the water's edge, I exchanged my cotton pants for chinos, and my T-shirt for a sweater. Then I descended the stairs, went out the front door, and switched on the porch light. Even then I couldn't see through the sluggishly stirring fog as far as the road. But when I pressed the flashlight's button the strong beam showed me not only the road but the edge of the potato field. I turned off the porch light and, guided by the flashlight's beam, went down the road and past the dune to the beach. Because I knew that damp sand would make for easier walking, I headed straight for the water's edge.

The flashlight's beam cut a tunnel of light, perhaps a hundred feet long, through the slowly eddying fog. At the beam's edge I could see the white froth of spent waves, sometimes flooding so high on the beach that I had to retreat to the softer sand to avoid getting my feet wet. At last, on impulse, I halted and switched off the flashlight. For a second or two I could see nothing but darkness. Then, gradually, my vision adjusted, and I saw that I seemed to occupy a little hollow scooped out of pearly, luminescent fog, a hollow that extended a yard or so in front of me and to either side. I took a few steps forward, and the hollow moved along with me. After that I kept the flashlight off. It was a delightful sensation, hypnotic and dreamlike, to walk in a moving cleared space in the fog, a space in which I was always the exact center. True, now that I could not see more than a few feet in any direction, the edge of a high-reaching wave sometimes washed around my ankles. But no matter. The water was warm. And it would have been worth more than that minor discomfort to experience this totally unexpected enchantment, and to feel, at least for a short time, that my anxieties, like everything else, were cut off from me by the pearly gray, eddying smother. I moved on for a quarter of a mile, perhaps more, aware of no sound except the breaking of waves on the offshore sandbar—now loud through the distorting fog, now soft—and the faint, plodding sound of my own footsteps.

And then suddenly there was another sound. A strange one, a kind of rhythmic squeaking, not far behind me in the fog.

Heart leaping, I whirled around, pushed the flashlight's button. Its yellow beam showed me a nightmare figure back there in the eddying mist. Someone tall, and clothed from hooded head to feet in shiny black. In the depths of the hood the face was only a pale blur.

For an instant or two both that black looming figure and I stood motionless. In that brief interval I had time to realize that the clothing—black rubberized waders with heavy rubber soles attached, rubberized jacket with deep hood—was that of a surf fisherman. But I knew, in every semiparalyzed nerve, that it was no innocent fisherman who had been trailing me.

I clicked off the flashlight. Unable to see anything at all, I ran to my right into the deeper sand. There were scattered houses behind the dunes along this stretch of beach. If I could reach one—

I heard the rhythmic squeaking, swifter now and at my left. The sound, I'd realized, was made by those rubberized legs brushing against each other. Suddenly I could see him, a blurred dark shape in the grayness. I whirled, ran to my right. The squeaking was very close now. Heart hammering, I changed direction again.

And then I was in water that reached almost to my knees and my attacker was upon me, fingers fastened around my throat, bearing me over backward into the water. I thrashed about wildly, left hand clawing at that slick shoulder. A nearly spent wave washed over us both and then receded with a sound of rattling pebbles, but the steely pressure on my throat did not slacken. In the increasing torment of my air-starved lungs I was almost unaware of the pain caused by those fingers biting into my flesh.

So this is what comes of it all, I thought. I'm going to die out here in the fog, without even knowing who my murderer is.

The flashlight! Why hadn't I thought before of the flashlight? Miraculously, it was still in my hand. As another low wave washed over us I managed to pull my right arm free. I raised the flashlight and brought it down as hard as I could on that hooded head.

Despite the effort I had put into it, the blow must have been a weak one and could not have hurt much, not through that hood. Perhaps it was surprise more than anything else that made that deadly grip slacken and the figure slump forward, its weight pinning me in the shallow water.

Desperately I wriggled free, got to my feet, thrashed through inches-deep water to the damp sand. I turned in the direction of that house beside the dune. If I again tried to cut across the deep sand in hope of finding some other house, that tall figure would almost certainly overtake me. This way I had a chance.

No sound of pursuit. Had I stunned him? Was he lying unconscious back there, with sea water already filling his lungs? Before I even knew I was going to I whirled around, pressed the flashlight's button. He wasn't drowning. He was getting up, already on hands and knees, and with the face in that deep hood turned toward me. Clicking off the flashlight's beam I turned and ran, aware that I had been a fool to stop even for that second or two.

Squeak, squeak. The swift rhythm of that sound told me that he, too, was running. Grimly, and despite my aching muscles and laboring lungs, I forced myself to a faster pace. I had a chance, I told myself. He had a much longer stride, but he was burdened with about fifteen pounds of clothing, and besides, I'd had a head start of perhaps a hundred feet.

Was the squeaking closer, farther away? Through the distorting fog, and with the blood pounding in my ears, I could not tell.

I ran on for several minutes. There was a sharp pain in my side now, and a continuous roaring in my ears, so loud that I could not tell whether the squeaking sound still followed me. Suddenly I knew that if I tried to keep running it would not matter whether he caught me or not. My heart would have burst, and I would be dead. I stumbled up onto the deep sand, sank to my knees, and then fell the rest of the way forward, cheek pillowed on my outflung arm. If he was still back there someplace, he might run past at the water's edge, unaware that I lay up here close to the dunes.

My laboring heart slowed. The roaring in my ears dwindled away. I could hear the wash of waves now, but no other sound. Had he given up, or was he, too, resting for a moment, only yards away in the fog?

The thought was enough to get me onto my feet. I did not return to the water's edge. I knew that by now I must be close to the dune behind which the house stood, and I did not want to risk missing it in the fog.

I kept on, half running, half walking in that ever-moving hollow scooped out of the mist. My right shin struck something and I went down, but I was glad of it because I recognized the obstacle that had tripped me up. It was a charred log, half buried in the sand, which must have served as a backlog for many a beach cooking fire. And the entrance to the dirt road that ran past the house was only a few yards ahead.

I listened. No sound except that of the waves. I decided to take a chance. I switched on the flashlight and swung its beam in a wide arc. Nothing. Nothing but sand, blue shadowed in the little hollows, and the lacy white of a wave's edge washing up onto the beach. Either he was quite far back there on the beach or, giving up, he had cut through the dunes to the potato fields beyond.

Nevertheless, I still moved at that half run as, guided by the flashlight's beam, I found the entrance to the road. I hurried up the walk and into the house, slamming the door and locking it behind me. I moved down the hall and into the lighted kitchen. Mrs. Conski stood at the sink, washing her supper dishes, and I realized with shock that it could not have been long since I left this house. It seemed to me that hours had passed. I hurried onto the little back porch, closed the door, and pushed its thumb latch into place.

Chapter 15

When I came back into the kitchen, Mrs. Conski was standing with her back to the sink, her broad face puzzled. "What you doin', missis?"

"Locking the house. Someone tried to kill me down there on the beach." The pain it cost me to speak reminded me for the first time of my bruised throat.

Aware that she followed, I went down the hall and into the living room and switched on the overhead light. I turned to her. "What do I dial for the police?"

She shrugged.

I went to the phone and dialed operator. I told her I wanted the police and she asked me where I was and I said near Quogsett. "Then I'll connect you with the Southampton Town Police."

A moment later I heard a man's voice. "Someone on the beach attacked me," I said. In answer to his questions I told him my name and phone number and the location of the house.

He said, "I'll send someone there right away."

I hung up. While Mary Conski stood watching, her usually stolid face inquisitive, I crossed to the sofa and sat down.

Somewhere not far away a car started up and drove off, the sound of its motor dwindling. I said, "Did you hear that?"

"What, missis?"

"A car driving off. It sounded as if it were somewhere on this road."

Excitement had made her almost loquacious. "No, I didn't hear a car, but then, I got to where I don't hear so good." She added, "You got marks on your neck."

I got up and crossed to a little gilt-framed mirror that hung on the far wall. Its surface, cloudy with age, gave back a dismaying image. My hair was wet and stringy, my face was pale, and my throat bore dull red marks that soon, surely, would turn black.

"I got to finish my dishes," Mrs. Conski said, and left the room. After a while I caught a glimpse of her through the archway as she moved along the hall to climb the stairs. But I felt that she'd be down again as soon as the police arrived.

I sat there, thinking of that faceless figure in black. Had he been some maniac, prowling through the fog? That was possible, but I did not think he was some madman, attacking his victims at random. I believed it was someone in whom I'd aroused an enmity, a deadly one.

I had angered several people since that rainy day when I had first opened Grace Woodhull's album. Which of them might have felt sufficiently enraged, or threatened, to try to choke me to death on a fog-wrapped beach?

Larry Philbeam was the first to come to mind, of course. The person who had stalked me, an unarmed young woman, through the fog, was both violent and cowardly, and both those traits were attributes of Larry Philbeam.

But it might have been one of the others. Beth Warren, for instance. I had never thought of her antagonism to me as down-right deadly, but perhaps it had become so. And certainly she was tall enough to be the figure in waders and hooded jacket. So, for that matter, was Doris Gowrey. But I did not think it had been Miss Gowrey. True, she was still erect and strong looking, and those big hands of hers might well have been the ones that had wrapped themselves around my throat. I doubted, though, that she would have been able to run in pursuit of me for several hundred yards.

But there were others who had resented my questions. Winstead Chalmers, for instance, and Gregory Woodhull. It was impossible, of course, to think of that old man in the wheelchair as my attacker. It was almost as hard to think of his beautiful and stately wife committing a violent act. But she had the physical capacity for it, and if for some reason I didn't know, she also had sufficient provocation—

I looked at my watch. A few minutes past seven. How long had I been waiting for the police? I couldn't tell, because I hadn't thought to look at my watch when I called them. But it seemed to me that it had been at least half an hour.

The minutes dragged by. I could hear, just barely, the muted sound of Mary Conski's radio. My guess was that she kept it low so that she would be sure to hear the police when they arrived.

They did not use their siren as they approached. However, I heard the engine, and so I had unlocked the front door and was standing behind the hooked screen when they stopped out front, dome light revolving. The fog was thinning. I could see not only the police car and the road but at least twenty feet into the potato field. As I stood there, I was aware of Mary Conski descending the stairs and crossing to the living room.

Two uniformed men were coming up the walk. With an uneasiness I could not have explained, I recognized the older and fatter one as Jim McPheeters, the policeman who had given me a summons for that incinerator fire. I unhooked the screen door and opened it wide. "Come in, please."

They followed me into the living room, where Mary Conski sat on a straight chair just inside the doorway. Jim McPheeters said, "You remember me, Miss Garson?" His eyes went to my bruised throat and then back to my face, but he made no comment.

"Of course I remember you, Mr. McPheeters."

"This here's another McPheeters, my nephew Ron."

"How do you do?" I said. The nephew was tall and freckled and seemed quite shy. He was turning his cap in his big hands as he nodded to me, smiling.

Jim McPheeters was looking at Mrs. Conski. "Hello, Mary." She nodded.

"I heard you were here," he said, and grinned.

With dismay, I understood the reason for that grin. Heard you were here, Mary, to keep an eye on that New York girl after that fire she denied starting.

I said, "Shall we sit down?"

We sat. Jim McPheeters said, flipping open his notebook, "Now what happened?"

"Someone tried to choke me. You can see that for yourself."

He gazed at my throat for a moment. "Bad-looking neck you got there. Be all black and blue in the morning. Now when and where did this happen? Here in the house?"

"No, on the beach, about two hours ago."

"On the *beach!*" He stared at me. "Why, the fog's still thick, and two hours ago you could cut it with a knife. And you went to the *beach?*"

The hands I'd clasped in my lap tightened their grip on each other. "I know it sounds strange. But I was feeling keyed up and restless, and when I went out to the backyard to hang up curtains on the clothesline—"

"You were hanging out curtains? In the fog? To get *dry?*"

My resentment flared. "I told you I was feeling restless. That's why I took the curtains down and washed them. I needed the work as—as a distraction. And I hung them outside because it is better that they be on the line, where they can start drying as soon as the fog lifts, than hanging damp in the bathroom overnight."

"Okay, okay. Go on."

"I'd just finished hanging up the curtains when I heard what sounded like a car stopping nearby. I thought of how I'd like to take a good long drive, but of course I couldn't in heavy fog, and then I thought of walking on the beach."

I leaned forward. "Because of what happened to me, I'm sure now that the car I heard had been parked not far from here along this road. I couldn't see it, of course, but it must have been close enough so that when I turned on the porch light, and then followed the beam of my flashlight down the walk and toward the beach, whoever was in the car was able to see me."

"Wait a minute," Jim McPheeters said. "Mary, did you hear this car?"

She shook her head.

"Maybe you were on the wrong side of the house to hear it."

Again she shook her head. "I was in the kitchen, with the window open. But I don't hear so good these days."

McPheeters looked back at me. "Go on."

I did, describing how I'd moved along through the fog, and heard that squeaking sound, and whirled around, with my flashlight's beam shining on that nightmarish figure. "Right at first, I didn't realize he was wearing a fisherman's waders and a rubberized jacket with a hood. But a minute or so after that—"

"Now wait a minute! Not many summer people buy a complete surf-casting outfit like that. It's mainly local fishermen who wear them. And I know all of them. Not one of them would do a thing like what you say happened, not one."

With difficulty I kept from shouting at him. "I didn't say he was a fisherman. I only said he wore the clothes a fisherman wears. For all I know," I said, with an extravagance I instantly regretted, "he could have been the Reverend Moon."

"The Reverend— You mean, you thought he was some kind of Oriental?"

"No, no! I don't know why I said that. I couldn't see what he looked like. He'd pulled the hood so far forward that his face was just a blur."

"All right. Go on."

I told of my struggle with the black-clad figure at the water's edge, and the blow I'd dealt with the flashlight. I told of my flight back through the fog, during which my pursuer had abandoned the chase, perhaps from exhaustion, perhaps for some other reason.

"When I reached the house I locked the front and back doors and then asked the operator to connect me with the police. I'd just hung up when I heard a car start up somewhere nearby and drive away. No," I added swiftly, "Mrs. Conski didn't hear it. She's already told me so."

McPheeters closed his notebook and dropped it into the right-hand pocket of his jacket. "Well, we'll go up the road after a while and see if there's some sign that a car parked there in the last few hours. Not that I think we'll find anything pointing to any particular car, not when dozens of cars park along the road every sunny day. Still, we might find something. But first let's go down to the beach. I want to see just where it happened."

"Good." Now he would have to believe that my attacker had worn fisherman's waders. Surely those thick rubber soles must have left distinctive prints in the damp sand.

He was looking at Mrs. Conski. "Want to go for a stroll on the beach, Mary?"

"Some joke," she said. "I'm going to bed." As the two policemen and I went out the front door, she was toiling up the stairs.

A breeze had sprung up. Only wisps of fog eddied over the potato field. Now, at past eight in the evening, there was more light than there had been in midafternoon. We walked past the dune and onto the beach. Only seconds later, I felt dismay. The tide had come in. The edge of a wave washed up the beach to within twenty feet of that half-burned log before it sank, with a seething sound, into the sand. That meant that the strip of sand, which for a time must have held my attacker's footprints and mine, was now under water.

Nevertheless, when the elder McPheeters said, "You say you went east?" I nodded and walked silently for perhaps a minute between the two men. Then I halted.

"This is completely useless, as I'm sure you realize. The tide is in. We'll see no tracks, or any other sign of what happened."

Jim McPheeters nodded. "That's what I figured. But I also figured it's up to me to prove that we small-town cops can be thorough, no matter what anyone says."

Had someone, perhaps some summer person, made a complaint about him, or otherwise given him a bad time? That might account for the chip on his shoulder.

"Well, we might as well go up and look at the area where you think you heard a car start up."

We tramped back over the deep sand through the fading daylight and then walked up the dirt road nearly to the wider paved road into which it ran. On the right-hand side the potato field came clear to the road's edge, but on the left there was a strip of about six feet before the plowed field began. The grass and weeds had been flattened by the tires of the many cars that had parked along here each sunny day since the warm weather began. But there was nothing, not even a fresh-looking cigarette butt, to indicate that a car had been parked here at some time during the last few hours.

In silence we walked back to the house and into the lighted living room. Jim McPheeters said, "You got any idea, miss, who tried to choke you?"

I had been waiting for him to ask that. "Yes. Larry Philbeam."

"Philbeam over Springs way? Oh, yes. I heard you'd been asking directions to his place."

Beth was right, I reflected. In small communities everybody did find out sooner or later, and usually sooner. "I wanted to show him an old album I found in this house. It had snapshots of him in it. He was asleep when I got there, but while I was talking to the woman he lives with he woke up and became—violent. In fact, he chased me in that old car of his until he piled into a tree."

"I heard about him hitting a tree, but I didn't know he was chasing you when he did it." He paused. "Why didn't you report that he'd been chasing you?"

"I was afraid that if I did he would become very angry indeed, and come after me. I thought that as it was, it was more than likely that he would not even remember anyone being at his house. I mean, he was that drunk. But maybe he did remember, and today—"

McPheeters turned to his nephew. "Ron, go out to the car and call Gully McLaren's patrol car over in Springs. Ask him to drive up Widow Winthrop's Path and check out where Larry Philbeam has been this afternoon. And ask Gully to call you back."

When his nephew had gone, I said, "Well, we might as well sit down." We did. A silence stretched uncomfortably. McPheeters got up and moved toward the bookcase. "Mind if I read something?"

"Not at all." I tried a feeble joke. "Maybe you'd like to read *The Sheik*."

The sharp look he gave me made me wish I hadn't made such

a silly-sounding suggestion. He took one of the half-dozen old *National Geographics* I had brought down from the attic and went back to his chair.

After a while Ron McPheeters came in. "Gully went to Larry Philbeam's shack," he said. "Old Larry was snoozing away. Birdie says he's been like that ever since around two this afternoon."

With a sense of bafflement I reflected that if Birdie would bail him out, she would also lie for him. But probably she had not lied, in this case. Probably he had been stretched out on that sagging double bed most of the afternoon, just as I'd seen him that morning. And even if he had been prowling around in the fog there was little chance that anyone had witnessed his movements. Surely no one would have seen him park along that narrow dirt road outside or follow me onto the beach.

I looked at the two men. Both of them were watching me with an odd mixture of curiosity and amusement and pity. In the younger McPheeters's face there was a touch of embarrassment, too. Before I realized I was going to, I burst out, "You don't believe a thing I've said, do you?"

"Now of course we do, miss," Jim McPheeters said. "How could we help but believe those marks on your neck? But, after all, the idea of old Larry dressing up in waders and jacket and trailing you through the fog— Why, I'll bet that in the last fifteen years Larry has never walked further than from his car into the liquor store and back."

"I didn't say it had to be Larry Philbeam! I just said it was someone."

"All right. Who else, then?" As I looked at him helplessly, he went on, "Why would anybody want to choke you to death, a nice-looking young lady like you? Why?"

I wanted to say, "Because maybe someone is not only angry with me but afraid of me, afraid I'll find out who committed a triple murder aboard the *Wave Dancer* twenty-five years ago."

But if I said that, McPheeters would say, "Who told you that what happened to the *Wave Dancer* and the people aboard it was anything but an accident? Who told you?" And anything resembling an honest answer to that would only heighten the look of amusement and pity I saw in their faces.

I said, "All right. So you don't believe me about the person in the waders and jacket. What do you believe happened to me?"

Jim McPheeters looked uncomfortable. "I don't know. But several times in my experience—well, a lady has an argument with her husband, or boyfriend, and things take a violent turn. Afterwards she's too embarrassed to tell the truth about her black eye or the marks on her neck, so she tells some story about hitting her eye against a door, or about some mugger coming up behind her and grabbing her around the neck."

I said, outraged and incredulous, "You think I went down to the beach to keep a date with some man, and he—"

"Doesn't sound too unlikely that you'd make a date to meet someone, does it? After all, you can't have much privacy in this house with Mary Conski here. And it certainly seems more likely that you'd be meeting someone down there than that you'd be walking through the fog all by yourself."

"But I didn't go down there to meet anyone!"

"All right, miss. You tell us who you think could have done this to you, since it sure looks as if it wasn't Larry Philbeam."

I looked at him helplessly. Oh, I could have given him names. The name of a chic woman realtor, and of the wealthy holder of a General Motors franchise, and of an embittered spinster, and of the rich Southamptonite she'd been in love with for so many years. I could have mentioned, too, the Southamptonite's beautiful second wife. But what motive—what motive that McPheeters would find credible, at least—could I assign to any of them?

I said bitterly, "All I'm sure of is that someone did it. Why, the way you act one would almost think you believe I tried to choke myself to death!"

Jim McPheeters looked embarrassed. "It's been known to happen. Wife of a cousin of mine, after they committed her to Rockland State Hospital—"

He broke off. I knew then, almost as clearly as if he had told me, that he had heard about the week I had spent at the Courtney-Latham Clinic. David, undoubtedly, had told Beth Warren.

She must have told her client, Doris Gowrey, and perhaps a few others. And from them the story had spread to everyone else.

Suddenly I saw myself through McPheeters's eyes. A young woman who had spent a week at a clinic for the nervous and mentally afflicted. A young woman who'd found something "strange" about her rented house, and whose incinerator had caught fire seemingly all by itself, and who had asked at the library for the name of a medium, and who now told some story about a person with a hood-hidden face attacking her on the beach.

In short, that crazy New York girl.

And perhaps, I thought bleakly, that was exactly what I was.

For the first time in many days I recalled the huddled figure I had seen—or at least thought I had seen—on the floor of my room on my last night at the clinic. Had she really been there? The next morning I had not waited to make sure.

If I had told Dr. Winestaff, instead of just a nurse, about that huddled figure, he might not have discharged me as "fundamentally sound." He might have decided instead that I was unsound indeed, unsound enough so that out there on the fog-shrouded beach today I might have been capable of hallucinating a figure in black, and then wrapping my hands around my own throat—

McPheeters said, still looking embarrassed, "Well, we'll certainly keep the case open. And if you think of anything else that could clear this up, you'll call us, won't you?"

I nodded mechanically.

"If there's nothing more we can do right now, I guess we'll go."

I saw them to the door, thanked them, and said good-night.

Filled with bleak purpose, I climbed the stairs. Tomorrow I would go to New York and to the Courtney-Latham Clinic. The woman on the floor in my room that night, I had decided, would be my touchstone. If I learned that such a disturbed creature *had* been wandering through the ward that night, I would conclude that my experiences in this house, too, had a reality outside myself. If, on the other hand, I learned that the woman could not have been real—well, I would consult Dr. Winestaff, and trust to him to see to it that, until I became well, I was not left free to complicate the lives of normal people, particularly not David Corway's life.

No sound came from behind Mary Conski's door. I continued past it to my own room.

Chapter 16

In the morning, inspecting my image in the mirror, I thought, thank God for turtleneck sweaters. I dressed in a cotton pantsuit of green and white checks, plus a sleeveless white turtleneck that hid the dark bruises on my throat. Then I packed the suitcase I'd brought with me to this house. As I moved toward the stairwell, suitcase in hand, I reflected that this might be the last time I would walk along this hall or descend these stairs.

In the kitchen I found I had no appetite for anything but coffee. I shook the percolator Mary Conski had left on the stove and heard a sloshing sound. Enough there for me. A few minutes later I washed and dried the cup and saucer I'd used and put them away. Then I picked up my suitcase and walked toward the front door.

Mary Conski sat on the porch rocker, her gaze fixed on the potato field now flooded with morning sunlight. As I came out of the house she turned and looked at my suitcase. "Going someplace, missis?"

I nodded. "New York."

"Be gone long?" As she spoke, her gaze was fixed on the neckband of my sweater. Plainly she was curious, not only about my destination today, but about what the police and I had said to each other after she went to bed the night before.

"Just overnight," I said. Unless, of course, I learned that the woman in my room at the clinic had not been real. In that case, I would never see this house again. I would call Beth Warren long distance and ask her for as much refund as she would give me. Surely she and Doris Gowrey, glad to be rid of me, would be willing to make a refund. And lord knows I might need the money, I thought grimly. Treatment at places like Courtney-Latham costs even more than summer rentals in the Hamptons.

She said, "Driving in?"

"No, I'll leave my car at the station."

At breakfast I'd decided that I felt too unstrung to drive a hundred and twenty miles. If I didn't return to eastern Long Island, I could phone the car rental people, and have their representatives out here pick up the VW.

I added, "Those curtains are still on the line." Those wretched curtains that I had hung out in the fog, thus confirming Jim McPheeters's opinion of my mental state. "Will you take them in later?"

She nodded.

"Well, good-bye for now, Mrs. Conski."

Again she nodded.

When I'd parked the VW with its nose almost touching the Bridgehampton station platform, I opened my purse and took out the train schedule, clipped from the East Hampton *Star,* to check again on the time of the morning train to New York. Suddenly I realized that this was Saturday, and the trains were therefore operating on a different schedule. The earliest train had long since gone, and the next one wasn't due for an hour. No wonder no one else was waiting, either on the platform or in the three or four parked cars.

I felt a chagrin out of all proportion to my mistake. Countless people must have made similar errors concerning train or plane schedules. But once others begin to doubt you, I reflected bleakly, or you begin to doubt yourself, every such mistake seems damningly significant.

Restlessly I got out of the VW and began to pace the station platform. Since the station was set well apart from Bridgehampton's business district, not many cars passed along the road paralleling the platform. A few did, though, perhaps heading for the electrical appliance shop a hundred yards or so farther on. The driver of one car, a woman with a vaguely familiar face, waved to me. I had no idea who she was. Perhaps I'd seen her behind the counter of some shop, or at the machine next to mine in the laundromat. It seemed to me that the occupants of some of the other passing cars gave me a certain amount of attention, but that idea, I realized, could have been the product of overstrained nerves.

The parking spaces were filling up now. People who for one reason or another had to leave the Hamptons for New York on this sunny Saturday climbed to the station platform, suitcases in hand. From somewhere to the east came the whistle of a diesel locomotive.

In midafternoon I stood at the reception desk on the Court-ney-Latham Clinic's main floor. What if the nurse who'd helped me pack that morning was no longer here, I thought, feeling my stomach tighten into a knot. What if no one here would know what I was talking about?

The well-coiffed, middle-aged brunette behind the desk smiled at me. "Yes?"

"I wondered if I might see one of the nurses, if she's on duty today. Her first name is Eileen, and I think her last name is O'Donnel, or something like that. She's short and red haired, and she's on the eleventh floor, or at least she was early in June."

"You almost got the name right. It's Eileen Donnely. And yes, she's on duty today. I think today is her turn at the nurse's sta-tion in the eleventh-floor hall."

Moments later, as I stepped out onto the eleventh floor, the el-evator doors sighed closed behind me. I could see Eileen Don-nely at her desk halfway down the highly polished corridor, red hair bright in the afternoon light slanting through the tall west window. Mouth dry, I approached her.

Her head lifted. She said, her face lighting up, "Why, hello, Miss Garson."

"So you remember me."

"Of course." Her smile began to waver. "You're not—back with us again, are you?"

"No." I added to myself, at least I hope not. "But I've been wondering about that woman who came into my room the last night I was here. Obviously she was quite—disturbed. While you were helping me pack the next morning you said that no one like that was supposed to be on this floor, and that you'd check to see what had happened."

She looked blank, absolutely blank. There had been no one here like that woman, I thought, with everything inside me knotting up, and so she had put the whole thing out of her mind.

Then she said, "Oh, yes! I remember now. *That* poor woman. Her being on this floor was just one of those mistakes that happen every now and then. She belonged in the disturbed ward, and that's where they put her along about daylight. Poor thing, she was suicidal."

I felt so weak with relief that I wished I had something to hold onto. I said, "What happened to her?"

"Oh, she's much improved. In some cases these antidepression drugs really work miracles. She's home with her husband now."

"I'm so very glad!" And I was. Relieved on my own account, I would have hated to hear bad news about that other woman, even though, to me, she had been just a huddled, anonymous shape on the floor.

"Thank you a lot," I added. "That woman's been on my mind, somehow." Eager to be out of that sad place, I looked at my watch. "Well, I'll have to say good-bye now."

Down on the street, with the sparse weekend traffic moving past and the tender young leaves on the trees looking almost transparent in the sunlight, I paused for a few moments. I'd left my suitcase in a locker at Penn Station. Well, it could stay there for the present. Right now I would go to the West Side brownstone that was home to both David and me. And because it was such a beautiful day, I would walk to Grand Central, take the shuttle train to Times Square, and then board the IRT train that would take me to the Eighty-sixth Street stop.

There was no really good reason for the lightening of spirits that I felt. The memory of that terrifying interlude on the beach the day before was still with me. What was more, I still had no idea of who my attacker had been. But at least now I felt sure that there *had* been an attacker, and that he had appeared just as I had described him to McPheeters. At least now I was convinced of my own sanity. Some might say that I had no right to be. But I had resolved to regard as a touchstone the existence or nonexistence of that woman who had invaded my room at the clinic. She existed, and therefore, I told myself, I had a right to believe in my own sanity.

The thought sharpened my eagerness to see David. The chances were excellent that he would be in his apartment at this hour. Over the phone he had said something about holing up to work this weekend. And I knew that in the past when he had worked on weekends he had preferred to do so at home rather than in his firm's otherwise-deserted offices.

I actually enjoyed that walk from the East River to midtown. Couples and family groups strolled along the wide sidewalk and moved in and out of shops devoted to clothing or hardware or antiques. Most of them had that Saturday look of enjoyment on their faces. Perhaps, I reflected, it is because New Yorkers set such a hectic weekday pace for themselves that on Saturdays and Sundays the whole vast city takes on an almost gala atmosphere of relaxation and pleasure. When I had descended the steps at Grand Central and gone through the turnstiles, I saw that the shuttle train was waiting. I boarded it for the brief journey to Times Square.

Because the IRT operates fewer trains on weekends, the platform was crowded with people waiting for the uptown express. Some of them had playbills from Times Square theaters in their hands. So the matinees were over. Anxiety seized me. In spite of what he'd said about devoting the weekend to work, David might be planning to go out to dinner tonight. In which case, he might not return to his apartment until late, and even then—painful thought—not alone. I considered finding a phone booth and telephoning him. But if I left the platform when the train was anywhere near, I would miss it. I made my way through the crowd to the warning yellow line about a foot from the platform's edge and leaned cautiously forward. Yes, I could hear it now from somewhere back in the tunnel, the roar of an approaching train.

And then something—someone—behind me propelled me violently forward and I was in the air, and the tracks were rising toward me, not swiftly, but slowly, slowly as in a dream sequence in a film. And then, aware of shock but not pain, I was on hands and knees between the tracks and I could hear shouts and a woman's scream and that other scream of braked steel wheels gripping steel rails. To my left there was a huge headlight bearing down, bearing down.

I don't remember turning around on my hands and knees, but of course I must have, because suddenly I saw the platform's wall rising from the tracks and two hands, one dark brown, one white, reaching down to me. I caught those hands and found myself drawn upward onto the platform. Gray mist was closing in by then, but I had a dim impression of my rescuers' faces—one white and middle-aged, the other young and haloed by an Afro—and of the train roaring into the station. Then, while nausea curled my stomach, the mist thickened and darkened and closed in around me.

When I swam up out of the mist I found myself lying on a bench against the station wall. Two policemen stood beside me. Beyond their blue uniforms I could see a small crowd of people with curious faces. One of the policemen turned away from me and said, "Go on, go on. Leave her alone. There's nothing more to see here." He turned back to me. "You want an ambulance, miss?"

Groggily I sat up. Aware of a stinging in my palms, I looked at them. They were reddened and bore small indentation marks. Gravel had done that, probably. One knee of my pantsuit was torn, and a little blood had seeped through from the scraped skin beneath. Otherwise, I seemed to be all right. "No, thank you. I'll phone a friend of mine and he'll—"

"Officer! You're not going to just walk away from this, are you?"

I saw then that not everyone had obeyed the policeman's injunction to move along. A thin brunette of about forty stood beside the bench. She wore horn-rimmed glasses and had an intelligent face, now filled with indignation.

"That was no accident," she went on. "I was standing right behind this girl. Someone shoved me, I fell against her, and over she went. No," she added, as if anticipating his question, "I didn't see who did it. My attention was, of course, focused on the victim."

I grew rigid. So someone had followed me, clear from the Hamptons. Someone who had seen me during that hour I had waited on the Bridgehampton station platform, or had heard from still another person of my presence there. I could imagine my pursuer driving to New York in order to be waiting when I emerged from the train at Penn Station, then following my taxi as I went to the clinic, still following as I walked through the Saturday strollers to Grand Central and caught the shuttle to Times Square—

"Look, lady," one of the policemen was saying, "accidents like this happen on crowded subway platforms. It doesn't mean that anybody does it on purpose."

Hazel eyes flashed behind the horn-rims. "Men!" she said scornfully. "Investigating this would mean a little more work, and you'd do anything to avoid that, wouldn't you?"

The policemen exchanged a look. "One of those," it seemed to say. "A women's libber. Probably a les, too."

The second policeman, stockier than his companion, spoke for the first time. "How do we investigate? You didn't see the one you say did it. You want us to put it on the six o'clock news that a girl skinned her knee when she fell off a subway platform, and that we're looking for anybody who might have seen somebody push somebody else?"

Without waiting for her answer he turned to me. "You think somebody did this to you on purpose?"

"Yes."

He looked taken aback. The woman said, "*Now* will you do this properly? Will you take her over to the police station and find out what she has to say? There's one right here in Times Square, you know."

"Yes, we know, lady. We work out of it," the stocky policeman said. He turned back to me. "Feel like you can walk now?"

I nodded.

The woman moved right along with us as we climbed the subway steps. Even before we reached the street I shrank inwardly at the thought of moving along the sidewalk with two uniformed policemen. But New Yorkers, thank heaven, particularly those who frequent Times Square, are used to all sorts of sights. I was aware of only a few second glances as, in my pantsuit with its torn and bloodied knee, I moved along with two cops and a determined-looking woman.

Inside the station house we walked past another policeman seated behind a tall desk, moved down a corridor, and then went into a small room furnished with a bare table and several straight chairs. A phone stood on the table.

The stocky policeman said, "Sit down, ladies. I'll send someone in to get your statements."

When he had gone I said to the other policeman, "Is it all right if I phone a friend?"

"Sure."

With an unsteady finger I dialed David's number. The phone rang three times, four. Just when, sick with disappointment, I had decided he wasn't at home, he said, "Hello."

I cried, "It's me. Diana. David, I'm—I'm in the Times Square police station."

"You're *where?*"

"The Times Square police station. Something happened on the subway platform. I—I got pushed off onto the tracks, with the train coming."

"Diana! My God!"

"I'm not hurt. Just shaken up. But could you come for me?"

"You're sure you're not hurt?"

"A skinned knee, that's all."

"Then hold tight. I'm starting right now."

I hung up. A few seconds later the door opened and a thin, youngish man in civilian clothes walked into the room. He gave me a brief smile, sat down between the woman and me, and opened a notebook. "I'm Detective Lanswood. Officer Kearney has told me about your landing on the subway tracks. Now first of all, what's your name?"

I gave him my name and my New York address. He took it down and then turned to the other woman. "And your name and address?"

"Marcia Stone." She gave an address on West End Avenue.

"You were a witness to this incident?"

"Very much so, in a way. It was because someone pushed me that Miss Garson nearly got killed. I fell against her, you see. But unfortunately I have no idea who it was who shoved me. Surely, though, you can find someone who did see who the person was." She glanced at her watch and gave an exclamation. "I had no idea it was so late. I must leave, right now. If you need to get in touch with me, Mr. Lanswood, you have my address." Her gaze went to me. "Good-bye, Miss Garson."

"Good-bye, and thank you very, very much."

For the first time, she smiled. "You're welcome. It's just that I get so darned sick of nobody ever doing anything about *anything*."

When she had gone, Detective Lanswood said, "Now Officer Kearney tells me that you, too, feel that somebody intended you to land in front of that train. Why do you think that?"

I drew a deep breath. "Because on the beach yesterday someone tried to strangle me. No," I added quickly, "I don't know who it was. There was this fog, and besides he was wearing a jacket with a deep hood."

I saw the expression I had expected to see—surprise, quickly followed by the poker-faced look of a man used to dealing with people who think enemies are directing death rays at them, or piping poison gas into their apartments.

"What beach was this?"

"A beach near Quogsett, in the Hamptons."

"You reported this to the police out there?"

"Yes, the Southampton Town Police. They sent two men to the house I've rented out there."

"Do you remember the names of the officers?"

I said reluctantly, knowing what would happen now, "They were both named McPheeters, Jim McPheeters and his nephew Ron."

He closed his notebook. "Excuse me for a few minutes, Miss Garson."

He went out. The uniformed policeman leaned against the wall, staring into space. I sat with my hands clasped in my lap, imagining what Officer McPheeters was saying over the phone to Detective Lanswood. "Poor girl's off her head. By now everybody out here knows she was in one of those clinics for nervous cases in New York. And since she's been out here—well, that business yesterday was just the last of the peculiar things she's done. Ask me, she knew damned well who made those marks on her neck. It was some man she's mixed up with, or else she did it herself, just the way she probably jumped down onto those subway tracks today."

Detective Lanswood came back into the room still wearing that poker-faced look. "Well, McPheeters told me all about it. He's continuing the investigation from that end, and we'll look into what happened here." He paused. "Are you going back to Quogsett right away, or will you stay in New York for a while?"

"I'm not sure," I said.

A more truthful answer would have been, "Perhaps neither." Because as I waited, hearing in my mind's ear the phone conversation between the two men, I suddenly had thought of another way I might possibly find out who he or she was, that person who hated and feared me enough to want me dead.

"Well," Detective Lanswood said, "either way you'll know the case is being kept open."

"Thank you." I got to my feet and so did he. "Would it be all right if I wait in the outside room? Someone is coming here to meet me."

"Of course. There's a bench just inside the main entrance."

Out in the larger room I saw that the policeman behind the high desk was now reading the magazine section of the Sunday *News*. As I waited on the bench beside the door, three scruffy-looking men, all in stained denims and cheap, short-sleeved sports shirts, came in off the street. Only the hangdog expression of one of them, and the handcuffs binding his wrist to that of the tallest of the trio, told me that one was a prisoner and the other two were plainclothesmen. The detectives greeted the policeman behind the desk and then led their captive down the corridor.

Only moments later David came through the door, his face taut with anxiety. As I got to my feet, he said, "Can you leave?"

"Of course." I felt a hysterical impulse to laugh. "Oh, David! Did you think I was under arrest?"

"I didn't know what to think." He grasped my arm. "Come on, I've got a cab waiting."

Almost as soon as our taxi started up Sixth Avenue, he put his arm around me, looked down into my face, and said, "Tell me about it."

"Please! I think I can tell you better in my apartment."

"All right," he said reluctantly. Then a look of shock came into his eyes. "Your throat! What happened to your throat?" He reached out and drew down the neckband of my sweater.

"I didn't know it showed."

"Just the edge of a bruise was showing." Face grim, but fingers gentle, he rolled the knitted material higher around my throat. "Now who did that to you?"

"I don't know. But I'll tell you all I do know about it when we get there."

We rode in silence for several blocks. Then he said, "You took the train into New York?"

"Yes. My car's parked at Bridgehampton station."

"You didn't bring a suitcase?"

"I left it in a locker at Penn Station. I figured I could take the subway down there later and get it. You see, I was afraid you might be going out soon, and I wanted to get to you before you did."

For answer, he tightened his arm around me. We didn't speak again until we reached our apartment house. He opened the double front door with his key. Two flights up, I opened the two locks on my apartment door with my keys. Because I had left the windows closed and the blinds down, the three-rooms-and-bath were dim and musty smelling. We moved through the apartment raising windows. At David's insistence, we washed the small scrape on my knee and covered it with an adhesive bandage. Then, back in the living room, we sat down on the sofa. He said, "All right. Now."

I told him all of it. How whenever I tried to learn more about what had happened that night twenty-five years ago off the Massachusetts coast I encountered reactions ranging from coolness to, in Larry Philbeam's case, violent rage. I told him of my struggle against an attacker in the fog, and of Jim McPheeters's obvious doubts of my story, and of my own terrible self-doubt, which had made me return to Courtney-Latham to try to learn whether or not the woman who had invaded my room that night had been real.

"When I learned that she had been, I felt better about myself, so much better that the thing I wanted most was to see you as soon as I could. I was waiting at Times Square for the uptown express when—"

I broke off, shuddering. His arm tightened around me. I said, "I remember the name and address of the woman who went with me to the station house. We could look up her phone number. She'd tell you that someone pushed her, and she fell against me, so hard that I—went over."

"You mean, I could check up on your story? Do you think I need to? I believe you." His voice was fierce. "How could I help but believe this"—he pointed to the torn knee of my pantsuit—"and this." He pointed to my throat.

With tears of relief and gratitude pressing against the back of my eyes, I said nothing. After a moment, David asked, "Are you going back to that house?"

"David, I feel I've got to."

He said, surprisingly, "I agree. We've got to find out who's trying to— I mean, if he's determined enough to follow you to New York, you can't find safety just by moving out of that house. But you're not going back there alone. I'm going back with you, and I'm going to stay with you."

"Stay! But your work—"

"I was to take my vacation in August. Instead, I'll take it starting tomorrow, and if my partners don't like it, they can buy me out. Don't worry," he added with a smile, "they won't want to buy me out. They need me too much."

His smile vanished. He asked, "Shall we take the morning train out to Bridgehampton?"

I hesitated. "David, while I was in the police station I thought everything over. I'm absolutely sure that everything that's happened to me is related to what happened aboard the *Wave*

Dancer that night. Now there's one person who was a witness to what happened."

"Beth Warren?"

I nodded. "You remember my telling you that story I read in an old issue of the East Hampton newspaper? About how, when the Coast Guard picked her up, Beth babbled some story about somebody stepping from a smaller boat onto the *Wave Dancer's* deck? While she was still in the hospital, she contradicted that story. In fact, she didn't even seem to remember telling it."

"Well?"

"What if she had a visitor while she was in the hospital? A visitor who caused her to change her story?"

As he looked at me, frowning, I went on, "I remember the name of that hospital in Boston. We could fly up there on the shuttle tomorrow."

"But after twenty-five years—"

"Surely someone is still there who was on the staff back then. And they'd remember the case, a child floating in the water near a burning boat. They might even remember whether or not some man or woman had come to visit her."

He said slowly, "I think you're right. Anyway, it's worth a try."

"Maybe we should catch the earliest shuttle. Then perhaps we might get back to New York in time to take the last train out to the Hamptons."

He nodded, and then gave a sudden grin. "Better not phone your Mrs. Conski or anyone else with the news that you're to have a house guest for the next month. Better just to present them with the good old *fait accompli*. If you'll give me the locker key," he added, "I'll run down to Penn Station and get your suitcase."

I gave him the key. He stood up. "Lock your door after me, both locks," he said, not smiling now. "And don't open it unless you hear my voice."

When he had gone I took a quick shower, put on a denim skirt and a fresh white turtleneck sweater, and then made myself a cup of tea. I carried it to the living room and sat there, sipping the hot liquid. Through the open window came that New York sound, which never quite dwindles to silence even at three in the morning, that sound made up of street traffic, and sirens close or distant, and the rumble of underground trains, and perhaps even millions of voices laughing, talking, crying. After the house beside the dune, where for many hours at a stretch there had been no sound but the wash of waves on the beach or the murmur of Mary Conski's radio behind her closed door, the continuous New York rumble seemed strange. In fact, this apartment seemed strange. But I felt safe behind my double-locked door, and both safe and comforted in the knowledge that when I walked out of that door tomorrow morning David would be beside me.

At last I heard his knock. I undid the locks and let him in. He said, setting my suitcase on the floor, "While I was coming back here on the subway it occurred to me that I'd feel a lot easier in my mind down there in that beach house if you and I share a room. But I suppose," he added wryly, "that your Mrs. Conski and your landlady would take a dim view of such an arrangement."

"So would Beth Warren," I said before I could stop myself.

"Beth? Why, Beth's no puritan." Then he smiled. "Oh, I see what you mean." He tilted my chin and kissed me. "But that was over long ago."

Chapter 17

The red brick hospital in Boston, on a street near the Charles River, had that prison look common to most large buildings—schools and factories and city halls—built late in the last century. Inside, though, it looked no more gloomy than any other hospital. Off to the right, visible through a wide archway, was a waiting room with magazines and bouquets of flowers on low tables, and chairs occupied by stoic-faced people staring into space. Straight ahead was the reception desk, with two young women, probably student nurses, standing behind it. As I walked with David across the floor's gleaming beige linoleum, I was aware that fear of disappointment had made my heartbeats uncomfortably rapid.

One of the nurses was brunette, the other blondish. I said to the blondish one, "I was wondering if you could give me the name of some staff member who was here twenty-five years ago."

"Twenty-five years! Wow!" She looked as if she herself hadn't been born until about eighteen years ago. "That's a long time."

"Miss Blake," the brunette said.

The blond nurse turned to her. "What?"

"Arlene Blake. She told me the other day that she came here in nineteen-fifty, right out of nurses' training school."

I asked, "And she's still here?"

"Is she!" the brunette said. "She's superintendent of nurses, that's all." She glanced at her watch. "Nine-fifteen. She'd be in her office now." She pointed with the pencil in her hand. "See that corridor? It's the third door down. It has her name on it."

As we moved down the corridor my heartbeats were still rapid, but with hope now. On the third door gilt lettering said, Arlene Blake, Superintendent of Nurses. In small letters underneath were the words, Come in.

In the outer office, a desk held a typewriter and telephone, but the chair behind it was empty. Through an open doorway I could see a woman in a white uniform seated behind a larger desk. I said, "Miss Blake?"

Her face, broad and handsome under gray-streaked dark hair and a starched white cap, turned toward us. "Yes?"

"May we see you? It's quite important."

"Of course." When we stood before her, she said, "Sit down, please," and gestured to the two straight chairs drawn up to the desk. A moment later, she asked, "Now what can I do for you?"

I said nervously, "I'm Diana Garson, and this is Mr. Corway."

"How do you do?" she said, and then waited.

I said, "Miss Blake, I understand you've been on the staff of this hospital for a good many years."

She nodded. "Around thirty."

"Do you remember a child, a girl, who was brought to this hospital one night in September twenty-five years ago? Her name was Elizabeth Bratianu, although later she was adopted by a couple named Warren. She had been found by the Coast Guard floating near the wreckage of a boat, a power cruiser that had caught fire and exploded."

"Of course I remember, poor little thing. Only she wasn't so little. Skin and bones, yes, but very tall for her age. I remember thinking, 'If this child keeps growing at this rate she'll be six feet before she's through.'"

David said, "You weren't far off the mark."

"Then she's all right?"

David nodded, and I said, "She's a real estate agent out on eastern Long Island."

"I'm glad. It was a miracle the child lived at all. Several people were lost aboard that boat, you know."

"Three people," I said. "A Mrs. Woodhull and her grown son and daughter."

Gaze sharpening a little, Miss Blake said, "Would you mind telling me, Miss Garson, what your interest in this matter is? You seem very young indeed to have any connection with something that happened that long ago."

Clasped hands tightening in my lap, I told the story I had rehearsed on the shuttle plane to Boston and in the taxi from the airport. "My mother was a close friend of Mrs. Woodhull's. She knew I was going to be here in Boston and so she asked me to visit this hospital. You see, my mother has never gotten over the idea that there was something mysterious about those three deaths."

"Mysterious? It's always mysterious when a boat goes down at sea with no survivors—or, as in this case, with only a hysterical child as a survivor."

"My mother feels it was even more mysterious than that. She has an old newspaper clipping about the boat going down. Maybe you don't remember, but in the first reports Beth was supposed to have said something about someone boarding the boat at sea, just before the fire and explosion."

"Yes, I do recall, vaguely. Didn't she say later on that she couldn't even remember saying anything like that?"

I nodded.

Miss Blake smiled. "The things children can invent! What's more, they sometimes believe them, at least for a while."

"Very young children, yes. But wasn't Beth a little old for such fantasizing?"

A certain stiffness came into Miss Blake's voice. "I'm afraid, Miss Garson, that I don't see what you're driving at."

I took a deep breath. "It's just this. I feel—I mean, my mother has always felt—that Beth was telling the truth when she spoke of someone boarding the boat. She feels that perhaps Beth had a visitor while she was here, someone who persuaded her to change her story."

"Visitor?" Miss Blake's voice was cold now. I could understand that. Protective of the hospital's good name, she resented the implication that someone could have gotten in to harass a child patient. "She had no visitors. Two Coast Guardsmen brought her in, and she saw no one but hospital personnel until several days later, when this couple came, the ones who intended to adopt her. I've forgotten their name, but didn't you say it was Warren?"

"That's right."

"She'd told us that these people, the ones who were to adopt her, were staying at some hotel in London. The Churchill, I think it was, although I certainly can't be sure after all this time. The hospital cabled them, and they flew back as soon as they could, although transatlantic planes were fewer in those days, and much slower."

I asked, "Were you one of the nurses assigned to her room or ward or whatever it was?"

"A room. A child who'd been through such an experience might have been a disturbing influence in the children's ward. Yes, I was one of the nurses caring for her."

I said, reluctant to offend her further and yet determined to learn all I could, "But of course there were other nurses, on other shifts. While you were off duty, some person might have—"

"Miss Garson! The whole hospital was interested in that child because of the circumstances under which she came to us. If she'd had a visitor, whatever nurse was on duty at the time would have told the rest of us. But, to the best of my recollection, there was a No Visitors sign on her door. I recall most definitely that newspaper reporters weren't allowed in to see her. They had to take whatever information the administration chose to give them."

But, I reflected, a hospital was a vulnerable place. Anyone could put on a white coat, sling a stethoscope around his neck, and go unchallenged almost anywhere. I thought of how Mafia groups, knowing that, placed their own guards outside the hospital room of a wounded associate who had escaped an attempt on his life.

But I mustn't say that to Miss Blake lest she order us frostily out of her office. I said, "I suppose you're right. But can you remember anything else about Beth's stay here?"

"Only that she was very distressed, and no wonder. She

seemed very attached to the people she'd been with, and they must have been very attached to her. One of them, the young woman— What did you say the family's name was?"

"Woodhull. The daughter's name was Sheila."

"This Sheila Woodhull had given the child a pendant in the shape of a gold squirrel, with chip rubies for eyes. Beth told us that it had been an 'ahead of time' birthday present. She was to be eleven in about two weeks. She became very upset when the nurse on duty—it wasn't I—tried to take it away to put it in the hospital safe, and so Beth was allowed to keep it in the stand beside her bed."

A gold squirrel with ruby eyes. I'd seen a pendant like that someplace, or a picture of it. In the album? Yes, that was where. Sheila had been wearing such a pendant in one of the last pictures in the album, a color snapshot of her seated at the piano.

"I can see how a child would love it," Miss Blake went on. "Still, I think it was an inappropriate gift."

"Inappropriate?"

"Too valuable. It was real gold, and rubies, even chip rubies, are not inexpensive. I remember that she was wearing the pendant when the Warrens took her away."

I waited for a moment, and then ventured, "Is there anyone else we could talk to? Someone who was here at that time?"

She said coldly, "I can't think of a soul. The doctor who attended her is dead now. The older nurses have retired, and the ones who were my age then have left the profession, or gone to other hospitals. And so, if you'll excuse me now, I have work to do."

David and I stood up, and thanked her, and walked out. Down on the street, in sunlight that had grown uncomfortably hot, David said, "Well, it was worth a try."

I wondered dispiritedly if it had been. We'd come all this way, and learned nothing except that Sheila Woodhull had given a skinny, almost-eleven-year-old a pendant.

Stepping to the curb, David raised his arm, and a cruising cab angled toward us. "Come on. Maybe we'll be able to make that last train out to the Hamptons."

Chapter 18

We did make the afternoon train, just barely. The air condition-ing was off in every car, a conductor told us. Perspiring in the heat—an even more intense heat than that we had encountered in Boston that morning—he seemed to enjoy telling us the bad news. But at least the train was not crowded. As it moved from station to station through Nassau County and western Suffolk, its old cars swaying and rattling over the uneven roadbed, it grew progressively emptier. By the time the train, running half an hour late, had moved through the villages and farmlands of east-ern Long Island, our car carried no one but ourselves. Exhausted by a long day of almost constant travel, I would have slumped against David's shoulder, except that the weather was too hot for physical contact. Sitting far over in the seat, close to a window with a star-fracture from some rock thrown in the past, I leaned my head against the back rest and closed my eyes. I did not open them until I heard the conductor call, "Bridgehampton."

We left the train. David put our suitcases in the back seat. "You drive," I said.

When he was behind the wheel, he turned his face toward me, heat pale under its tan. "Where shall we have dinner?"

"At the house," I said promptly. With the summer season in full swing, and on a night as hot as this one, every halfway de-cent restaurant would be crowded. I hated the thought of waiting in line. Better to have something simple, like a salad and cold sliced ham, from the refrigerator at the house.

We drove through mellow sunset light, past well-spaced houses and stretches of farmland, to Quogsett. Even though Beth's red Datsun was not in front of her office, I of course thought of her and of that unrewarding interview with Arlene Blake in Boston. When David turned onto the road leading toward the ocean, though, my thoughts shifted to the old house beside the dune. Even with the sea that close, the upstairs rooms would be uncomfortable on a night like this because the house had no insulation. Well, it couldn't be helped, and later tonight cooling breezes might spring up. We turned left onto the paved road running parallel to the dunes and then onto the narrow dirt road that led directly to the house, standing brown and smallish and ordinary-looking in the last of the daylight. As we parked beside it, I saw Mary Conski's face, a white blur in the dusk, looking down at us from the window of her room.

With David carrying both suitcases, we entered the house through the unlatched back screen door. "Wow!" he said.

"It'll be even hotter upstairs," I warned.

It was. We placed my suitcase in my bedroom and his in the smaller room almost directly across the hall and then retreated to the ground floor. In the shadowy kitchen I turned on the dangling overhead light and opened the refrigerator door.

Surprise and dismay held me motionless. No small ham with only a few slices gone from it. No almost full jar of mayonnaise. Nothing but a half-loaf of whole wheat bread in its transparent wrapper and, in the door's egg compartment with its oval indentations, two small brown eggs. Not only my food had disappeared, but the link sausage and mound of hamburger, food that belonged to Mary Conski and that I vaguely remembered seeing in the refrigerator before I went to New York. I knew Mrs. Conski hadn't taken my food. She was conscientious about not touching any groceries I bought, and expected me to treat her purchases with equal respect.

"Had to throw things out," Mrs. Conski said from the doorway into the hall. "Power failure."

That wasn't surprising. Power failures resulting from extreme heat or cold, or high winds, or cars colliding with utility poles, are one of the hazards of life on eastern Long Island. I straightened up. "When?"

"Before noon yesterday. Didn't come back on until about an hour ago."

"What did you do about your dinner tonight?"

"Went to my sister's in East Hampton. Power stayed on there."

I said to David, "I guess we'll have to go out to a restaurant after all. I don't think there are any stores open this late."

"Pilaski's," Mrs. Conski said.

I looked at her inquiringly. "Pilaski's Delicatessen in Hampton Bays," she said. "Open till midnight in the summer."

I frowned. Hampton Bays was about twenty miles away. I said, turning to David, "If you like, we'll go to a restaurant. But if you'd be willing to drive to Hampton Bays while I unpack my own things and make up your room—"

"Why not? What do you say we make a picnic of it? Carry our deli stuff down to the beach where it's cool."

David has his faults, heaven knows, but irritability isn't one of them. Many men, after the sort of day we had spent, would have exploded at the thought of a delicatessen meal, particularly one prefaced by a long drive through heavy Sunday night traffic to get the ingredients. He accepted the idea, not only with good grace but even with enthusiasm.

Mrs. Conski, usually so fond of her own company, lingered in the doorway while David and I discussed the menu for our impromptu picnic. We decided upon assorted cold cuts, Swiss cheese, and cucumber salad in place of the desiccated lettuce and spotty tomato I had found in the refrigerator's vegetable compartment. "And I'll browse around," David said, "and buy anything else that looks good."

"Don't browse too long. And oh, before you go, let's look in the album. The pendant," I added, in answer to his inquiring glance, "that little gold squirrel."

"Oh, yes. The one Beth was wearing when they brought her to that hospital in Boston."

Mrs. Conski stepped aside, and David and I moved past her

down the hall to the living room. I switched on a lamp, opened one door of the bookcase, and drew out the album.

"See?" I said a moment later.

Sheila Woodhull, wearing a blue evening dress and seated at the piano, smiled up at us. Around her neck was a pendant in the shape of a little gold squirrel with red eyes. I felt a ripple down my spine. The first time I saw her—or imagined that I saw her—as I stood at a point halfway down the stairs, she had been seated at the piano. And although I couldn't recall seeing the pendant, I did remember that her dress had been blue.

"That must be it," David said, "the one the nurse told us about."

"I wonder if Beth still has it."

"Probably, although I've never seen her wear it. It doesn't seem her style, somehow. Well," he added, "I'm off."

We turned. Mrs. Conski stood out in the hall, just beyond the archway. David said, "Can I get anything for you at the deli?"

"I do my own shopping," she said, and turned to the stairs. They creaked under her weight as she climbed. David looked at me, eyebrows lifted, and I smiled and shrugged.

"It's nothing personal," I said in a low voice. "Just moral outrage. I think she's realized that you are going to be here at least overnight, and maybe longer."

"Point out that she'll be our chaperone."

"I will, but I doubt it will make her feel differently."

"Well, tell her that I'm here, and that I'm staying. Now keep the doors locked until I get back from Hampton Bays."

"Oh, David! In this heat?"

"Well, keep the screen doors locked. And if you hear anything, slam the inner doors shut and lock them."

When he had gone I replaced the album in the bookcase and went upstairs. The door of Mary Conski's room was closed. Probably she had gone to bed. I certainly hoped so.

It took me about five minutes to make up David's bed with sheets and two light blankets. Then I crossed to my room. As I lifted my suitcase onto the bed, I learned that Mary Conski had not retired, after all. She said, from the doorway, "Is he staying all night?"

"He's staying for a month." At her dumfounded look, I quickly added, "He'll have his own room."

Her expression said, as plainly as any words, that only about eight feet separated my bedroom door from that of the one across the hall. Aloud she said, "Mrs. Gowrey won't like that. Beth Warren won't either. It ain't in your lease that you can have a man stay here."

"It's not in my lease that *you* can stay here." Then I checked my annoyance. If Mrs. Conski moved out in righteous indignation, Doris Gowrey would have all the more reason to insist that David's presence was grounds for eviction. "Please, Mrs. Conski. I assure you that his being here won't make any difference."

She snorted. I'd never heard her make that sound before.

My nerves snapped. "Mrs. Conski, I need a man's protection! You know that. You know what happened on the beach Friday afternoon. And yesterday in New York—"

I broke off, and then said in as calm a voice as I could manage, "Please, Mrs. Conski. We'll talk everything over tomorrow. I'm very tired tonight. And I want to shower and change my clothes while David is gone."

Not answering, she turned and walked away down the hall.

About ten minutes later I emerged from the bathroom, refreshed by my shower, and wearing the coolest thing I owned, an off-the-shoulder dress of pale yellow cotton. I looked at my watch. David couldn't be back for at least an hour, and if he did browse along the delicatessen shelves, or if the New York-bound Sunday night traffic was exceptionally heavy, he might be gone considerably longer than that. I hadn't yet finished unpacking my suitcase, but I'd leave that for now. It was still too hot to stay up here any longer than necessary. I walked toward the stairs.

I halted. There was a note affixed to the closed door of Mary Conski's room with a piece of transparent tape. She had written with a pencil on lined paper:

> Missis,
>   Going to my sisters place in East Hampton. Missis
> Gowrey don't anser so I foned [she'd scratched that

out and substituted phoned] Beth Warren about that
man. I fealt I shood.

Yrs. truly,
Mary Conski.

Saw sin, reported same. Well, both Doris Gowrey and Beth
Warren soon would have learned about David anyway. I went
on down the stairs.

In the lower hall I hesitated. It was only a little cooler down
here. I walked to the door, snapped on the porch light, and
looked through the screen. The porch light's glow, with small
white moths dancing through it, reached clear to the narrow dirt
road. Unable to resist the promise of cooler air, I unhooked the
screen and went down the porch steps to the road. If I saw anything or heard anything I could dash back into the house and
slam and lock the door in nothing flat.

I looked up. A few of the major stars, drowned-looking, shone
through the haze. I turned toward the beach. A faint breeze
blew past the dune and stirred the damp hair on my forehead.
Lovely! If David and I held our picnic close to the water's edge
we might even get a little fine spray from a wave now and then.
Until he came back, of course, I wouldn't dare go down to that
dark beach. But the glow from the porch light dimly illuminated
the dune beside the house. If I climbed up there, I could get the
full benefit of that faint breeze from the sea—

The sound of a car. I whirled around. To judge by its headlights, the car approaching along the dirt road was a small one.
David in the VW? No, it was much too soon for David to be
coming back. Heart suddenly hammering, I turned and dashed
up the walk and the porch steps.

"Hey! Diana!" It was Beth Warren's voice.

I turned. It hadn't taken her long, I thought wryly, to react to
Mary Conski's phone call. As I started back down the steps the
red Datsun stopped, its lights shining on the dune for a moment
before she switched them off. She got out. Her reddish-brown
hair, like mine, hung damply around her face, but otherwise, in
her pale blue cotton shirt and full matching skirt and brown

espadrilles, their ties laced up around her tanned calves, she looked her usual chic self.

She said, smiling, "Who did you think was coming? The vice squad?" She added quickly, "Just kidding. But Mary Conski did phone that a David Corway had moved in, only she called him Carraway."

"Yes, she left a note saying she'd phoned you."

"Doris Gowrey isn't going to like this, you know, not one bit. I thought the three of us should talk over how best to handle her."

It was apparent that Beth planned to behave in a friendly fashion. For the first time I was glad that she and David once had been lovers. Plainly she didn't want to cast herself in what would appear to him as a disagreeable role.

I said, "He isn't here right now. He went to Hampton Bays."

"Mary Conski told me that, too. When she's sufficiently worked up, that woman can be downright chatty. But I don't mind waiting until David gets back."

"All right," I said, and turned toward the house.

Beth groaned. "Do we have to wait in that uninsulated hot box?"

"Of course not. I was just about to climb up onto the dune. It would be much cooler up there, and we could see David's lights when he turned onto this road."

"Good thinking, as they say in those TV commercials."

We walked to the dune and, feet sliding, climbed to its crest. I sank onto the sand, legs curled around me, and she sat facing me, dimly illuminated by the refracted glow of the porch light. It was pleasant up there. I could feel the faint breeze, and hear the lazy wash of waves. Turning my head, I saw that beyond the dry sand, pale in the darkness, lay a faintly gleaming swath of wet beach. The tide was out.

"So you and David went to that hospital in Boston."

Startled, I swung my gaze back to her. "How did you know—" Then I realized how. Mary Conski had been standing in the living room doorway while I held the opened album, and David and I discussed the squirrel pendant with the ruby eyes.

"Yes, we did go up there, Beth. I know you must hate our rummaging around in the past, particularly since it holds painful memories for you. But things have been happening to me, things that I can't help thinking are connected with what happened twenty-five years ago to the Woodhulls."

No need to say what things. By now surely she—and plenty of other people—knew that I'd told Jim McPheeters about a murderous attack upon me in the fog. By now, also, there had been time for news to spread of that Times Square detective's call to McPheeters.

"David and I, we—we thought that maybe the first story you told after the Coast Guard rescued you was the true one. We thought that maybe someone *had* climbed over the rail of the Woodhulls' boat that night, and that later he'd come to the hospital and frightened you into changing your story.

"Our trip up there turned out to be a wild goose chase," I went on, "but we thought it was worth a try. I hope you don't mind our going there."

"Mind!" She added in a completely unamused tone, "God, that's funny."

As I sat in bewildered silence, she rushed on, "Why have you been so stubborn? Why didn't you move out of that house to that other one I offered you? Oh, not that I believe in your spooks, but you do. And because of that crazy notion of yours about the Woodhulls you've kept snooping and snooping—"

She broke off for a moment and then went on, "God knows, at first I tried to get you out of there without hurting you. That incinerator fire, I mean. I knew it would give Doris Gowrey grounds to evict you. But that didn't work."

I said, slowly and incredulously, "I thought that perhaps you'd lit the incinerator. But are you telling me that after that—"

"I decided I had to get rough? Exactly. I had to. You were still snooping around, asking questions of Doris Gowrey and Win Chalmers and Larry Philbeam. You were driving me crazy."

I said, still not really believing her, "You mean that last Friday on the beach it was you in those waders and jacket? You mean you went out and bought—"

"No need for that. The waders and jacket had been hanging in the garage of a house that's on my summer list. A real lemon. I haven't rented it once in the four years I've been showing it.

Anyway, when I woke up Friday morning, hating you as usual, the fog was terribly thick, and I thought of that surf-fishing outfit, and what a perfect disguise it would make in heavy fog or at night. Well, by midafternoon the fog was the thickest I've ever seen."

I heard her voice going on and on, telling how she'd driven to that empty house and changed to the waders and jacket, and then, inching her way through the murk, started driving toward the beach. When she'd turned onto the dirt road that led to the house beside the dune, she'd turned off her headlights.

"I parked close enough so that I could see a blurred glow from the kitchen window. By five thirty, I knew, Mary Conski would have finished her supper and dishes and gone up to her room. I intended to go in the back way and make some sort of noise. When you came into the dark kitchen to investigate, I'd hit you over the head with a tire iron. Oh, not hard enough to kill you. Just hard enough to give you a bad scare. But then, as I waited there in the car, I saw the porch light go on. Then I saw the beam of your flashlight, angling first across the road and then toward the beach."

She had followed me, first by the diffused glow of my flashlight and then, after I turned it off, by the dim shape of my body. She stumbled over something, perhaps a piece of driftwood, and dropped the tire iron. Afraid she would lose me if she stopped to look for it, she got to her feet and kept following.

"As I said, I hadn't meant to kill you, but when I got my hands around your throat and started squeezing—" Her voice had thickened. She broke off and then said in an almost sullen tone, "If I'd been able to catch you after you hit me with that flashlight, I would have killed you."

I looked at her sitting there in the darkness, a tall, chic woman with her long legs curled around her. Still with that half-incredulous bewilderment, I wondered why she was telling me all this. Surely she hadn't forgotten that sooner or later David would come driving down that road. Surely she realized that I would tell him and the police all that she was telling me.

That sullen voice went on, "The next day I hated you even more, if possible. I was just coming out of the drugstore in East

Hampton when I met this woman who works on the *Star*. She said she'd seen you at the Bridgehampton station, waiting for a train that wasn't due for almost an hour.

"I didn't have any particular plan in mind while I drove to New York and waited for you at Penn Station. Mainly, I just wanted to see what you were up to. For all I knew, you intended to hire a private detective. Anyway, I followed you in another taxi to that clinic and then stood waiting across the street until you came out. Plainly, you were too high on some sort of good news to notice that I followed you from across the street, not directly across but a little way back." She paused, and then said, "There in the subway station it seemed too good a chance to miss. You were leaning out over the—"

She broke off, body stiffening, eyes staring past my shoulder. Even in that dim light I could see that her face held a blend of angry dismay and alarm. I twisted around.

A few hundred feet down the beach the beam of headlights cut through the dark, shining on pale dry sand with its shadowed blue hollows and, beyond that, on a strip of wet sand and the white froth of a low, incoming wave. Someone had driven down another of the rutted roads that led across potato fields to the beach and parked there at the road's end.

I heard the distant slamming of car doors. After a few seconds a man and woman appeared, moving slowly along the beam of light that shone over the sand. Even at that distance I could see that they were both elderly. The white-haired man appeared thin except for the paunch stretching the waistband of his almost knee-length red swimming trunks. His stout companion, head covered by a white bathing cap, wore a full-skirted black bathing suit that reached to mid-thigh. They'd left the car lights on, I realized, to help insure their safety as they crossed the driftwood-strewn beach.

Just an elderly couple, who perhaps had found themselves unable to sleep on this sweltering night and thought a dip in the sea might help. Why should their arrival have caused Beth anger and dismay?

Suddenly I knew why, knew it with cold, sick certainty.

I knew, too, why Beth had felt it safe to boast of how, unsuspected, she had made those two attacks upon me. She intended that I would be unable to repeat her words to David or anyone else.

Momentarily paralyzed, I stared at the figures moving cautiously toward the water. They wouldn't stay in it long. And after they returned to their car, after they drove off, leaving me alone with Beth—

Should I try to get to my feet and run toward that frail pair, crying out for whatever help they could give me? But what if Beth had brought a gun with her, or a knife? Maybe she hadn't, though. Maybe she had felt that she, taller and stronger and heavier than I, could once again just wrap her long hands around my throat—

Best not to take the chance she wasn't armed, I warned myself. And don't let her know you've guessed. Best just to try to keep her talking until you can think of what to do.

My neck felt rigid as I turned my head to face her. I saw then, with a wry thankfulness that seemed to squeeze my stomach into a knot, that it had been lucky for me that I hadn't tried to scramble to my feet and run. She had a gun, all right. Doubtless she'd carried it in a pocket of that voluminous skirt. Now it rested on her knee, its metal gleaming faintly, its muzzle pointed straight at me.

She said in a calm voice, "Don't scream, and don't move. As long as you sit there quietly you won't get hurt."

No, not until that elderly couple had left. And when they had? I pictured her forcing me to move, at gun point, down through the loose sand of this dune to the beach. And a split second after a bullet smashed into the back of my head, she would turn and race toward the road and the red Datsun. Would she, I wondered with a weird detachment, get rid of the gun by dropping it in one of the numerous ponds that dot the eastern Long Island woodlands? Maybe not. She was arrogantly self-assured, so much so that she had delayed her final attack upon me so that she could have the pleasure of letting me know about the two former ones. Anyone that arrogant might risk keeping the gun.

I managed to move my lips. "Why? Why do you want me dead?"

"Didn't I just tell you that you'd be okay as long as you sit there quietly?"

I ignored that. "It's because of Winstead Chalmers, isn't it? You're afraid that somehow I'll find out the truth about him."

"Truth? What truth?"

"That he was the one who boarded the *Wave Dancer* that night and set fire to it, maybe—maybe killing the Woodhulls first so that they couldn't send out a call for help—"

She gave a short laugh. "Winstead, a murderer? Win the Wasp, the upwardly mobile, the oh-so-respectable?" Then, in a cold, even voice: "You're right about one thing. The Woodhulls were dead before the fire started. But there was no one else aboard except me."

For an instant, in the shock of her words, I forgot my own peril.

I said, "But you couldn't have. You were only a child."

"You think children don't kill? You should read a book or two on the subject. Anyway, I wasn't your ordinary almost-eleven-year-old, not by a long shot. I'd lived through plenty. All those uncles who came to our lousy apartment to sleep in my mother's room, while I slept out on the couch. Some uncles were there for months, others only for a night. The things I could tell you about those uncles, especially an Uncle Bert—"

She broke off. In the silence, unbroken except by the gentle wash of waves, I stared at the gun and thought of that bathing-suited couple, perhaps still moving cautiously over the wood-strewn beach toward the water.

Again Beth was speaking in that bitter voice. "The children's home was even worse. At least before I'd had my mother's protection, more or less. But the home was old and dirty and overcrowded and understaffed. A group of the toughest kids ganged up on every new kid who came in. It was a kind of initiation. And if you blabbed they made it twice as rough for you from then on.

"Then the Warrens showed up, and liked me. I looked the way a favorite cousin of hers had as a child, Mrs. Warren said. They took me out to the Hamptons for the summer on trial, so to speak. Then Dr. Warren decided that they should go to London for the convention. I'd probably enjoy a cruise to Maine with her friends the Woodhulls, Mrs. Warren said, more than staying in a London hotel. So I went with the Woodhulls."

Again she fell silent. I longed to turn my head, just enough so that I could see those two down the beach, see if they had entered the water or—terrible thought—had started to emerge from it. But I did not move.

She was speaking more rapidly now. "There were three cabins on the *Wave Dancer*. Mrs. Woodhull and her daughter Sheila had the largest one. Her son Derek had the next largest, and they put me in the smallest.

"On the second day of the cruise, while Derek was at the wheel and Mrs. Woodhull and Sheila were up on deck, I slipped into the largest cabin and looked into Sheila's jewel box. Down at the bottom I found what I was looking for, a beautiful little golden squirrel with red eyes. I'd wanted that pendant terribly ever since the first time I'd seen her wear it. I put it back in her jewel box, but after that whenever I thought it was safe to I'd slip into that cabin and hold the squirrel in my hand for a few minutes. When we anchored for a few days in Bar Harbor, Sheila went to parties given by friends there, but she didn't wear the pendant. On the return trip south I decided that she had forgotten she had brought it with her. If it disappeared from her jewel box, she wouldn't miss it now. And if she looked for it after she got home, she'd figure that someone had gotten into the house and stolen it. And so I opened her jewel box one afternoon and took the squirrel and hid it under the mattress of my bunk.

"Maybe Sheila had planned to wear it when we stopped at Newport. Anyway, she missed it from her jewel box, and then both she and Mrs. Woodhull started looking for it and they found it under my mattress. Mrs. Woodhull told me she'd have to tell her old friends the Warrens what I'd done. Not to tell would be doing them a wrong, she said."

All the bitterness came back into Beth's voice. "Can you imagine how I felt? The Warrens had been more than a little doubtful of me as it was. That was why they had taken me on trial for the summer. If the Woodhulls told them I was a thief they would never adopt me. I'd go back to the home, where the kids who'd given me a rough time would give me an even rougher one now, because before I left I'd bragged about the rich people —not that the Warrens were really rich—who were going to adopt me."

She paused. I looked at her through the dimness, seeing not just her but, in my mind's eye, that old couple down the beach. My neck seemed to actually ache with that need I mustn't give in to, the need to turn my head and see what they were doing.

Beth said, "We'd been stopping at marinas each night all the way to Maine, and also on the way back. But two days after Mrs. Woodhull and Sheila found the gold squirrel under my mattress, something went wrong with the boat's engine. A broken fuel line, I think I heard Derek say. Anyway, it was early evening by then, and we were miles from the marina where Derek had intended to stop, so he put a kind of canvas-and-metal thing over the side—a sea anchor, he called it—and rigged lights to warn other vessels that we'd broken down. By a little after nine, we'd all gone to bed.

"There was a shotgun, a repeater, hanging on the alleyway bulkhead. The Woodhulls used it for skeet shooting. Derek had showed me how to use the gun, and how to load it. And so later that night—"

I heard myself cry softly, "No!"

"Yes!" She leaned forward slightly, and it seemed to me, although in that dim light I couldn't be sure, that her finger tightened around the gun's trigger. "You were so damned determined to find out what happened aboard the *Wave Dancer*. Well, now you're going to know."

That couple, I thought numbly. They must still be there, or Beth would not still be talking. Were they swimming in the trough between the first and second line of gentle breakers? Sitting on the wet sand at the surf's edge and letting spent waves wash around them?

Beth was saying, her voice matter-of-fact now, "I waited until I was sure they were asleep. I went into the alleyway, where a dim light was always left burning, and took down the shotgun and went into the gallery, where Derek kept the box of ammunition in a drawer. After I'd loaded the gun I went into his cabin and walked up close to the bunk. I shot him once in the back of the head and maybe twice in the body, but the first shot must have killed him because he didn't move afterward. When I went back to the alleyway I saw Sheila coming out of the large cabin. I shot her, oh, maybe twice, and then I stepped across her and used the rest of the shells on Mrs. Woodhull as she was trying to get up out of her bunk. Then I laid the shotgun on Sheila's bunk and went to her dressing table. I took the little squirrel pendant from her jewel box and clasped its chain around my neck."

Again the horror of what she was saying erased momentarily the sense of my own danger. I stared at her, seeing not this tall woman, sitting very erect in her chic clothes, but a monstrous child, standing in the midst of carnage while she clasped a pendant—a pendant that had cost three lives—around her neck.

"I went up on deck," Beth said. "Along the afterrail there were lockers holding life preservers, a spare anchor, rope, an oil lantern, things like that. There were also several five-gallon tins of gasoline. I put on a life preserver. Then I carried two tins of gasoline, one in each hand, down into the alleyway between the cabins. I drenched everything with gasoline—the deck, the bulkheads, furniture, everything. Then I took matches from the galley up onto the deck, and lit the oil lantern I took out of a locker. I carried the lantern to the top of the companionway and threw it down into the alleyway. It broke, and flames spread all over. I ran to the afterrail. I waited until I was sure that the fire was burning so well that there was no chance of it going out. Then I slipped over the side and swam away.

"Oh, I was scared of the black water, and it was cold, too. But I knew that we were close to shore, and that there must be other boats not far away, and that one of them would see the fire.

"And then I saw that already there was a boat close by, too close. It was smaller than the *Wave Dancer* and it showed no lights and its engine wasn't running. I was terrified. I knew that whoever was aboard that boat must have heard shots. They'll pick me up now, I thought, and take me to the police. But they didn't. The boat's engine started up and it moved away, still without lights.

"But I knew that I must have a story, in case the people on

that boat later on told what they'd seen and heard. It was then that I thought of saying some stranger had come aboard the *Wave Dancer* and killed the Woodhulls and set fire to their boat and then, before he left, tossed me into the water. I knew that I could keep the story vague and rambling. That was the way they'd expect someone my age to sound after a bad experience.

"I don't know how long I'd been in the water when the fire got to the fuel tanks and the boat blew up. Flaming bits of stuff came raining down out of the sky. I felt pain in one arm and shoulder and knew that I'd been burned and started screaming. Then a searchlight shone across the water, and soon there was a lifeboat beside me, and men in uniform were hauling me out of the water.

"After a few days in the hospital I realized it would be best to change my story. I'd asked the nurses every morning and again in the evening if anyone like somebody on another boat, for instance, had said they'd seen the *Wave Dancer* catch fire, and always the answer was no, there'd been nothing like that in the news. And from talk I'd overheard between the doctors and nurses I knew the Woodhulls' bodies hadn't been recovered, and probably never would be. There are deep fissures in the continental shelf along that stretch of coast, and boats and fairly large ships have been lost without a trace.

"And so when one of the doctors sat down beside my bed and told me that the Coast Guard and the police wanted to know if I had remembered anything more about the man who boarded the *Wave Dancer*, I acted as if I didn't know what he was talking about. When he explained, I told him that I didn't remember telling the men who rescued me anything like that. I couldn't remember much of anything about that night, I told him. I remembered going to bed in my cabin and I remembered floating in the water near the burning boat, but I remembered nothing in between. The doctor patted my hand and told me no one would be allowed to bother me with any more questions and I should just try to forget the whole thing and get well.

"My skin grafts took, and after a while I went home with the Warrens, and soon after that they adopted me. Until now," she said bitterly, "things have gone quite well for me. Oh, I've wanted a few things I didn't get. David Corway as a husband, for instance. But on the whole, it's not been bad. Then you came along, prowling, snooping—" Her voice trailed off.

I thought desperately, that old couple. Surely they weren't still in the water. Had they carried robes over their arms as they moved along the swath of light? I couldn't remember. Perhaps they had. Perhaps now, snug in terry cloth robes, they sat side by side on the dry sand. Perhaps they talked quietly. Or perhaps they sat in the companionable silence of the long married, watching the lazy curl of waves for a few minutes before they drove off toward their bed—

For a moment the impulse to run toward them, screaming, was almost irresistible. But of course Beth would shoot me down before I'd moved a yard. Oh, she didn't want those two as witnesses, not if she could help it. But still, they would constitute no great danger to her. Before they could reach the spot where I lay, she would have driven off. And even if their aging eyes caught a glimpse of her through the haze-dimmed starlight, it might be hard for them afterward to say even whether the tall figure in some sort of pale garment had been that of a man or woman.

And anyway, I thought bleakly, after all she had told me, she *had* to try to kill me.

A sudden thought brought me a momentary flare of hope. Maybe someone else would drive down to the beach, either along the road the elderly couple had used, or, better yet, along the one that led to this tall dune. Someone who might, after all, be able to save me. Several carfuls of young people, say, bringing with them firewood, six-packs, a record player, and all the other ingredients of a beach picnic. But even as the thought crossed my mind, I knew that beach picnics didn't start this late. As for lovers, they usually sought the privacy of the Long Island woodlands. And as for David—well, David must be still miles away, driving along a highway crowded with weekenders who had delayed their return to heat-baked New York as long as possible.

No, I thought, dry-mouthed, all I could do was to try to keep her talking, hoping that somehow, someway—

I tried, and failed, to keep my voice from shaking. "You say I've snooped. But with all my snooping, I'd never have found all this out if you hadn't told me. And Beth, I won't tell anyone else—"

"Of course you won't," she said calmly. "You won't be able to. But as for your not finding out any other way, I think you might have. For sheer persistence—" She broke off and then said, "Why, I heard that you even visited a medium in Riverhead." When I didn't speak, she added, "You did, didn't you? What did she tell you?"

"She said that she couldn't tell me anything."

Could it be that Irene Fell *had* seen what had happened aboard the *Wave Dancer* that night? Was that the "heavy" thing she didn't want "to mess" with? Certainly she, mother of that lovely young girl in that photograph, must have felt horror indeed at the thought of an even younger girl's cold-blooded slaughter of adults who had befriended her.

I forced myself to speak again. "Anyway, I didn't think you believed in things like that."

"Of course I don't believe in anything like that!"

Again with a strange detachment I thought, "Don't you?" Just as she had on other occasions, she had avoided going into that house tonight. Was her reason just that on the dark beach, where I would have no chance to get to the phone or to seize some weapon to use against her, she would find me easier to handle? Or was there still another reason why she hadn't wanted "to wait for David" inside that house?

"It's just that your visiting a medium," she said, "showed the lengths you'd go to. And listen!" She leaned toward me. "I don't know anything about whoever was on that other boat that night twenty-five years ago. People on the wrong side of the law, almost surely. Maybe they'd stolen the boat. Maybe they had an illegal alien or two aboard. But if they're still alive, it means that somewhere in the world today there are men who heard those shots and saw me standing at the afterrail until the fire got big, and then slip overboard."

"And you thought that David and I might somehow find out about that other boat, might track down the men who'd been aboard it? How could such an idea even have occurred to you?"

"It never occurred to me that you'd go to that hospital in Boston, but you did! It never occurred to me that anyone, after all these years, would learn about that gold squirrel, but you did. When Mary Conski told me tonight that she'd seen you and David looking in that album and talking about a squirrel pendant Sheila Woodhull was wearing in one of the photographs—well, I knew that I couldn't stand it any longer. I couldn't stand waiting for you to wreck my engagement to Win, wreck my whole life. I knew I was going to have to kill you, and to make certain of it this time.

"That damned squirrel," she said broodingly. "The Warrens kept talking about how fond of me Sheila Woodhull must have been to give me an ornament like that. Finally I felt I had to get rid of the thing. So one day, when the Warrens and I were at the beach—this very beach, as a matter of fact—I accidentally on purpose wore it in swimming. When I reached the deep water I unfastened the clasp." She turned her head to look at the water, faintly luminous in the starlight. "Unless somebody found it, and I doubt that anyone did, it's still out there someplace."

Her face was still half-averted. If I could launch myself at her, seize the gun—

But before I could gather my courage, her face turned back toward me. And then I saw, from the way her body stiffened, that the old couple were leaving. Even in that dim light I could see the slow movement of her eyes as she followed their progress across the beach. Stomach knotted, blood drumming in my ears, I heard the distant slam of car doors, heard an engine start up. I could imagine the car backing, then turning, so that its lights no longer stabbed toward the water.

The sound of the car's engine dwindled away.

"All right, Diana," she said evenly, "on your feet. We're going down toward the water."

I'd known she'd say that. She wouldn't want to leave me lying up here, in full sight of someone who, before she got well away from here, might come driving down this road.

"Beth, listen to me! If you kill me, you'll be found out." Praying she wouldn't notice, I let my hand slip, palm downward, from my knee to the sand.

"Now why should I be found out? Did anyone find out who followed you along the beach that day? Did anyone find out I was on that subway platform?" Keeping the gun pointed at me, she got to her feet in one smooth motion. "All right, Diana. Stand up."

If I was to save myself it would have to be now, right now. Once she had that gun at my back I'd have no chance at all. Awkwardly, one fist balled, I got to my hands and knees and then stood up, bringing with me a handful of beach sand. I flung it into her face.

She cried out. Almost simultaneously I heard the gun's report and also heard, or thought I did, the whine of an object past my cheek. I turned and plunged down the dune, feet almost sliding from under me. Again there was a shot, and again I heard, or imagined I did, the whine of a near miss.

I turned, running, onto the walk that led to the lighted porch. From the corner of my eye I saw that no headlights moved along the paved road that ran at right angles to the narrow dirt one. But even if I had seen lights, and even if they had been David's, he would have been too far away to help me, because now I could hear the pound of her footsteps behind me on the walk.

I raced up the porch steps. I heard another shot and the sound of a bullet striking the door frame. With a wild surge of hope I recalled that most handguns held only six bullets. If that was true of hers, she had already spent three shots. I was inside the house now. No time to try to turn and slam the door and lock it, because by then her long legs had carried her up onto the porch.

I plunged up the stairs toward the landing, dimly illuminated by its overhead light. From behind me came the sound of her stumbling at the foot of the stairs. On that first riser? On a worn spot in the old stair runner? I didn't look back but just raced on, grateful that I had gained a precious second or two.

At the landing I turned left. No locks on any of the bedroom doors. The bathroom? No! Its lock was only the flimsy hook-and-eye kind. I was sure she could burst the door open by running against it. Better my own room. If I could wheel that heavy chest of drawers across the door—

As I turned to dash through the doorway of my room I saw her on the landing, the gun in her raised hand. I heard another shot but felt nothing and thought with hysterical thanksgiving that sand in the eyes made for poor marksmanship. By then I'd slammed my bedroom door behind me. Dimly aware of my sweat-drenched body and pounding heart, I began to push the chest sideways to block the door.

Beth screamed. The sound was high-pitched, prolonged.

I heard two more closely-spaced shots. Then again that scream, so filled with hopeless terror that my fear of her was replaced by another fear, a nameless one that made the hair stir at the back of my neck.

No more shots. But then, I realized, probably the gun was empty now. And no more screams. Just a terrified mewling that sounded scarcely human. The mewling noise seemed to diminish, as if she were backing away toward the open doorway at the far end of the hall and the narrow balcony beyond. Sure that she could not hurt me now, I stepped out into the hall.

She was out on the balcony, her back pressed to the railing, and that useless gun in her hand. Her face, dead-white and with distended eyes, was almost unrecognizable. She seemed to be staring, not at me, but at something or someone beyond me. The impression was so strong that I turned to look. I saw nothing but the dimly illuminated hall.

Beth screamed again. I turned around. Now her gaze seemed focused on something between herself and me, something visible only to her.

I saw the tall body press back even farther against the railing. Then, overbalanced, she toppled. I heard her drawn-out, despairing cry, and felt pain in my bruised throat, and knew that I was screaming, too.

My legs gave way and I crumpled to the worn hall carpet. I don't know how long I huddled there, aware that I should go out and look over that rail, and yet unable to force my muscles to obey me.

The sound of a car stopping outside. Sound of the front door opening, and David's voice, calling my name. I heard the pound of his footsteps on the stairs, and then he had drawn me to my feet and into his arms.

To this day, I don't remember what I said in those first moments. I only know that sometime later I found myself seated on the top step of the stairs. David was saying, "Wait here. I'll go see."

He went down the stairs. I heard his footsteps along the hall to the rear door. After a few minutes he was back at the foot of the stairs.

"She seems to be still alive." His upturned face was very pale. "She fell into that old cement pool, with the gun still in her hand. Just sit there, darling, while I phone for the police and an ambulance."

He went into the living room. Shaken and sickened as I was by the events of the last half hour or so, I still had room for awareness of something else.

Those three weren't there any longer. I don't mean merely that I felt they were cut off by some kind of barrier. They weren't there at all.

Now this was just a commonplace house, just another Hamptons summer rental, filled with the battered funiture and anonymous atmosphere of a place where, over the years, scores of people had lived for a few weeks or months.

Chapter 19

We'd had to wait in line at the Marriage License Bureau. (As David remarked, one would think the month was still June, not July.) Consequently, when we emerged from the Municipal Building the rush hour had begun and there seemed to be no cabs available. At my suggestion we took the IRT uptown express.

Now, as we stood in the crowded car, both of us hanging from straps, I could see a headline on the tabloid held by a fat man seated in front of me. It read: "Young Boy Held in Slaying of Two."

Not that I needed headlines to remind me of Beth Warren. For a while I'd thought of almost nothing except her and her death, which occurred about twelve hours after she had been taken to Southampton Hospital.

Although she had a broken neck and internal injuries, she was conscious when they brought her in. And she insisted upon talking—to the doctors, the nurses, the seventh squad detectives from Riverhead, the orderlies, and anyone else who would listen. According to the detectives, her talk had been disjointed, jumping from subject to subject and back and forth in time. She'd talked of me, and of the children's home, and of that night aboard the *Wave Dancer,* and of someone named Uncle Bert, and of me again, and of a little gold squirrel with red eyes.

Somehow the detectives sorted it all out. At the inquest I had only to confirm that the things she had said in the hospital were much the same as those she had told me while she sat facing me atop the dune, with a gun resting on her knee.

At one point the coroner said to me, "Apparently just before the deceased fell she was hallucinating. In the hospital she said" —he consulted his notes—"that she saw 'all three of them' moving toward her along the hall. Do you know anything about that, Miss Garson?"

I said, "All I know is that I saw no one in the hall." Which was the truth, as far as it went, and that was as far as I intended to go. I did not want to talk about those three.

I have thought of them, of course. Particularly I think of those days when, like one drugged, I had a dreamy sense of living in the Woodhulls' time, a simpler, easier time than my own. But I feel no nostalgic yearning to relive such moments in that house. Now, when I think of those days, I feel what I was only vaguely conscious of then. I feel those responses—the ripple down the spine, the stirring of hair on the scalp—which my body made, perceiving a danger that my bemused mind did not.

During the week that David and Mrs. Conski and I lived in that house, I had no sense of presences other than our own. Yes, Mrs. Conski came back to the house. Having made her moral point, she returned the next day. She was still there when David and I left for New York, minus the partial refund I had hoped to obtain. Doris Gowrey, to use a phrase of my Aunt Gertrude's, had made a poor mouth. Beth Warren's death there would make the place hard to rent, she said, and besides it was late in the season to get a new tenant. Consequently, I didn't try very hard to get my refund. As David says, what the hell. We've got enough ready cash for a two weeks' honeymoon in Vermont. And just think of the money we'll save paying rent on one apartment —his—rather than two.

I looked around the subway car, filled with New Yorkers who, as usual during July and August, were at their unloveliest. Balding men in mesh sport shirts with chest hairs sticking through. Women with loaded shopping bags held upright between their bunioned feet and heavy legs. I saw an unprintable graffiti in red

46

paint above one of the car's doors. (Except, of course, that someone *had* printed it.) I saw a teenager with long blond hair holding a transistor radio to his ear, even though the sound blasting from it—not "Harbor Lights," or "I'll See You Again," but "Don't Jive Aroun' with My Woman"—may have been audible in the next car.

And I loved what I saw and heard, all of it. This was my own time, noisy and complex and dangerous and frightfully fast moving, but challenging and exciting, too, and I loved it.

David said, looking down at me, "Why the smile?"

"I was thinking how happy I am to be Diana Garson."

"And here I had the distinct impression that you liked the idea of becoming Diana Corway."

We both leaned to the right as the train, wheels screeching, rounded a curve. "You know what I mean. I'm happy to be me. Right now. Right this minute, standing beside you and hanging from a strap in this awful subway car."